The Whisper of Glocken

The Whisper
of Glocken

CAROL KENDALL

Illustrated by Imero Gobbato

A Voyager/HBJ Book
HARCOURT BRACE JOVANOVICH, PUBLISHERS
San Diego   New York   London

Library of Congress Cataloging-in-Publication Data
Kendall, Carol, 1917-
The whisper of Glocken.
(A Voyager/HBJ book)
Summary: Prompted by a terrible flood, a seemingly
unheroic group of little people sets out on a quest to
restore an ancient treasure and make the valley of the
Watercress safe again.
[1. Fantasy]   I. Gobbato, Imero, ill.   II. Title.
PZ7.K33Wh   1986   [Fic]   85-17634
ISBN 0-15-295699-9

Printed in the United States of America
A B C D E F G

To Silky Star,
sometimes known as
Gillian

The Whisper of Glocken

1

And in this land between the mountains shall our folk safely dwell so long as the Watercress flows from Snowdrift through Frostbite.

—Gammage, ancient prediction recorded in the Scroll of Time. Translated by Walter the Earl for *Glorious True Facts in the History of the Minnipins from the Beginning to the Year of Gammage 880.*

Spring came late to the Land Between the Mountains in the year of Gammage 885. Once arrived, however, it made a tremendous splash. Torrents of rain sliced into the twelve villages along the banks of the Watercress River. Rain slopped down on Watersplash at the head of the river and cascaded on Water Gap at the foot, where the Watercress dashed foaming through the underground passage in Frostbite. And it poured equal shares on the ten villages between.

There had been nothing like it in the lives of the Minnipins, or Small Ones, since that day when Gammage led his people into the valley 885 years ago. At that time the rain had been their salvation, so folk could only regard the present downpour as a good omen, though admittedly very damp.

After two days and nights of nothing but the gray slant

of rain, when every nose poked outside turned into a water-spout, the sun rose heroically blazing over the Sunrise Mountains, and villagers from Watersplash to Water Gap burst from their damp thatched cottages like trout after a green fly. As the mayor of each village hastened to post the Season's Proclamation, there was nothing but joy and rejoicing within the peaceful valley. Spring was upon them at last.

In eleven of the villages there wasn't the faintest hint of disaster to cloud the sunlit sky. But in Water Gap, even before the sun touched the bell tower, there were signs and portents to be read had anybody stopped to read them. Nobody did.

Crustabread, who dwelt alone on the left bank, the low side, of the river, should have been the first to notice that all was not well with the Watercress. But Crustabread was not at home. On slipping away from his solitary cottage at first light, he had noticed that the sarcen field was flooded, but he concluded that Scumble had left the sluice gate open.

From the edge of the opposite, higher bank, Scumble himself should surely have noted the flooded field and sounded the alarm, for he had done nothing so daft as to open the sluice gate. But he had something else on his mind that morning. He was cleaning his fish-press.

The fish-press would always reek of fish, just as his house always reeked of fish, and just as Scumble himself always reeked of fish, but it was an honorable reek. When the wintry sun sulked behind clouds from dawn to dusk, then folk were happy enough with the strong stuff which he bottled for them—the pressings of the minuscule oil-fish. They didn't hold their noses *then*. Oh no. For then they reeked of fish too.

Scumble whistled in time to his scrubbings and scrapings. Voices from the market square carried clear, and the peals of Glocken's chimes every quarter-hour hung on the sparkling air.

The chimes flurried into sound now, like a shower of dewdrops disturbed by a bird. Scumble chuckled deep in his throat. Caught dreaming again, that Glocken. Late with his peal. Ever since Plumb the Mayor brought back that History-Scroll from the Year Meeting, Glocken had been downright unreliable as a bell-ringer. He forgot everything, once he put his nose in that scroll. It was written by somebody in Slipper-on-the-Water, Walter the Earl by name, and had a long title, *Glorious True Facts in* something or other. . . .

Picking up the last tone of the chimes with his whistle, Scumble laid his brushes and scrapers in the sun to dry and went inside to wash his hands. It was time to go down to the river to inspect the moorings for his nets.

When Glocken finished chiming out the half-hour on the silver bells that hung everywhere about him in the tower chamber, he was prepared for the twits and jeers from the villagers below him in the market square.

"Heigh, Glocken! Stay awake up there!"

"Stop dreaming on village time. Do it in your bed at night!"

"Ho, Glocken! How many Mushrooms did you slay between the quarter-hours?"

"The only Mushroom that Glocken ever slays is with his teeth at dinner!"

The jibes were good-humored this morning because of the sun, but Glocken almost preferred folks' anger to their laughter. What did they know of the adventure and romance of history, these butchers and bakers and fish-oil-makers? Scarcely one of them had troubled to read for himself about the glorious battle against the dreaded Mushrooms. And yet, just two villages up the valley, in Slipper-on-the-Water, lived great heroes: the illustrious Walter the Earl, that wise woman Muggles, the painter of marvels Curley Green, clever Gummy, and fearless Mingy. Their very names shot forth sparks of radiance like the blue-white flame of the storied swords of the Minnipins.

Glocken still felt a shiver as he remembered that night five years ago. He was only a twig at the time, but even then he spent most of his hours in the bell tower, learning the chimes and the peals against the day when his old father would ring his last change. He liked to look down on the rest of the world, and though the trees obscured much of the view, he could see a few high points beyond his own village.

On that night he had crept up to the bell tower after dark, and he had seen a radiance off toward the Sunset Mountains. Now he knew what the radiance was, for he had read Walter the Earl's account of that splendid battle with the Mushrooms.

The swords, heavy and dull, grew warm in the hands of the brave Army of Fifty and began to glow with an inner radiance. The glow became a glimmer and then a shimmer. Suddenly the swords burst into blue-white flame and the words of the ancient writing stood out in burning letters: *Bright when the cause is right.*

Bright when the cause is right . . . !

The vision of flaming swords slowly dissolved and became the old familiar silver bells hanging above his head. Glocken sighed and brushed back the lock of hair that had fallen over one eye. Not for him or his likes the journeyings and adventures of a Walter the Earl or a Muggles. He was firmly tied to the telling of time and to his life amongst the dull villag-

13

ers of Water Gap. Reluctantly he rolled up the wonderful reed scrolls that told of the Minnipins from the ancient days on the Golden Mountain right down to the stagnant present.

With a warning creak the great time wheel approached the three-quarter mark and Glocken dutifully lifted the mallets out of their sockets. Then, while he waited for the wheel to make its final turn, he wandered over to the riverside window.

So clear in his mind's eye were the half-dozen puddles of yesterday that for several moments he couldn't see what his eyes were staring at. When it finally got through to him, he threw up his arm as though to shut out the sight.

A sheet of silver stretched across the sarcen field to the very edge of the trees beyond. Water lapped at the foundations of Crustabread's house, standing lone and forlorn on the opposite bank.

The time wheel tinkled. Mechanically, Glocken tapped bells with mallets to declare the three-quarter hour, but all the time his mind was tumbling and twisting over and around the problem of the flooded field. Down in the market square green cloaks fluttered in the sun. Should he sound the alarm? No. The master of the bells, stated the ancient rule book, must ring the tocsin only in moments of extreme danger when all else has failed. And perhaps—perhaps after all it was only that Scumble had left the sluice gate open.

He must summon Scumble then. No need to consult the Peal Book for the sluice-gate keeper's ring. He knew the Peal Book by heart.

> *To summon Scumble to the door,*
> *Chime Two, chime Four, chime Two once more.*

He struck the Two-bell a mighty whack, then Four-bell, and Two again. So that there could be no mistake, he rang the summons three times more.

He took another look out of the riverside slit. Was it his imagination, or had the water risen since his first look? What was keeping Scumble? Was the wretch now trying to close the sluice gates? But even as he thought it, Glocken knew that no sluice gates could account for the silver sea that was the left bank.

When finally the swift pat-pat came from the stairway, Glocken had no need to see him to know that it was Scumble. When you are a presser of fish, the precious oil gets under your fingernails and behind your ears and works its way through the fibers of your clothes to your skin and so into the very fiber of *you*, until you smell unendingly and oppressively of fish. There is no more mouth-watering smell than fish when it is in a fish, but transferred to a human being, it makes the nose draw back. Particularly on a warm day.

The sluice-gate keeper burst wheezing into the bell chamber. "I was just on my way to the Mayor!" Scumble's usual well-oiled tones had gasps and chokes. "It's the river, Glocken! In full flood! And more coming. . . ." He flung himself down on a stool and heaved and hummed to get his breath back.

Glocken felt oddly relieved. Naturally and of course, it was only a flood. How had he got hold of such ominous thoughts? It was true he had never seen a flood before that covered the whole sarcen field and beyond, but a flood was a known thing, a reasonable thing. There was no need to act as though the Mushrooms had attacked the valley.

"Should I sound the alarm?"

"I don't know. I just don't know." Scumble wrung his hands. "No, not yet. . . . It's just . . . and the Mayor. . . . I must see. . . ." He jerked himself toward the door, his eyes like pebbles squeezed out of two holes in a white sack. He disappeared from view and then thrust his head back into the tower chamber. "Stand by, Glocken!" he croaked. "It may be up to us to save Water Gap!"

But the heroic words were spoiled by the jutting head, the pursed mouth, the bulging eyes. Scumble looked for all the world, just then, like a wall-eyed pike about to take the worm. Glocken sighed as the pike swam down the steps. The only thing Scumble would ever save was the oil from a fish head. Why should Water Gap have such ridiculous folk in it when Slipper-on-the-Water had brave adventurers like Walter the Earl? In Slipper-on-the-Water, Walter the Earl had raised an Army of Fifty from ordinary villagers—an Army of Fifty that marched to battle at a moment's notice, though none had ever before wielded a sword.

Imagine any of the folk of Water Gap marching any-where at all! Scumble, whose smell of rancid fish might make an enemy flee holding its nose . . . pompous old Thick, the miller . . . pathetic little Goober, who had never grown all the way up, but grew outwards until he measured the same in all directions, like an outsize kickety ball. Or Furz the Tailor, or Warp the Weaver with his hunched-over back.

Glocken shrugged. It was fated. The very beginnings of Water Gap were inauspicious for heroes, for it was here that the sick and infirm had been left while the rest of the

Minnipins traveled on up the valley—all except Glocken's ancestor.

Though the family of the first Glocken had arrived safely, he himself had never got through the tunnel of the dried riverbed but had perished outside, probably washed away when the flood came. All that remained of that first Glocken was the Whisper Stone, a poor enough remnant of an inglorious end.

The Stone was lodged in a wall niche of the bell chamber, placed there, so the story went, by the son of that first Glocken and never since disturbed. It was just a rough fragment of slate with scratchings on it, like a homemade charm. Nobody knew exactly what the Whisper of Glocken was, though the Pretend-stories handed down through his family claimed it was some sort of bell with mystic powers. But who could believe family Pretend-stories? They were for entertaining children.

Brushing the hair from his eyes, Glocken took another look at the sarcen field. The water was still there, lapping at Crustabread's house. He suddenly wondered about Crustabread. Shouldn't he be summoned across the river? If the flood got worse, his house would soon be window-deep in water.

But even as he turned to the bells, he realized that it was hopeless. If Crustabread hadn't already crossed the Watercress to the high side, he would have to stay where he was. Nobody could cross now without being swept through the tunnel by the current. . . .

By the current. . . . Frowning, he turned back to the window, not quite knowing what it was that struck him as

17

odd about the scene. Where the Watercress was wont to flow placidly toward the wide tunnel mouth, there was now a great sploshing and foaming of waves. But . . . somewhere inside him a bird began to flutter. The waves . . .

The waves were breaking in the wrong direction!

In the 885 years since Gammage had brought his people through the dried-up river bed into the valley, there had been more than one flood. But always the river flowed south. "And in this land between the mountains," said the ancient prediction of Gammage, "shall our folk safely dwell so long as the Watercress flows from Snowdrift to Frostbite."

But the Watercress was no longer flowing from Snowdrift to Frostbite. The fluttering of bird wings inside Glocken grew to a dreadful flapping.

The Watercress now flowed from Frostbite to Snowdrift.

2

With the snide of the serpent
And the glide of an eel,
The water comes sliding
At Minnipin's heel.

With the tumble of the pigeon
And the grumble of the grouse,
The water comes bumbling
Into Minnipin's house.

With the cunning of the Brush-tail
And the stunning wit of toad,
Minnipin comes running
Up the river-road.

—Gummy, *Scribbles,* Volume **Two**
(Collected Works)

Unlike Glocken's remote ancestor, the first Crustabread
had made it safely inside the valley, but in a deranged state
of mind. Or so the tale went. He and all the Crustabreads
after him had the Quirk.

The original settlers had thrown up shelters on the low
bank of the Watercress, where they landed. Later, as the
first Gam Lutie nursed them back to health, they built their
clay and reed-thatch cottages on the high bank—all except
the first Crustabread. Against all coaxings and cajolings and
advice, he stuck to the low bank, and all the Crustabreads
after him had done likewise. In time the villagers had

learned to let them alone. Somehow, there was always a spouse to be found on the high bank to share the mysterious Crustabread existence. But the present Crustabread was mateless and lonely, for since the death of his own folk, he had had nobody.

When he started off from his cottage at first light of that fateful day, he had to pick his way with care along the ridge that marked the sarcen field. The water had never stood so deep, but now that the rain had stopped, the Watercress should quickly return to its banks. Probably by the time he got back from the Burying Place, there would be only soggy spots.

Padding softly along the trail, he arrived at the Place by midmorning. The stones were piled up just as he had left them. Crustabread fetched a few more rocks from the nearby stream and added them to the others. Then he sat down crosslegged and tried to remember what his life had been like when his father and mother were alive.

From earliest memory he had lived the warm days in the open, watching the birds and the busy woodmice, learning the secrets of the gray scampers high in the trees, drinking in the knowledge of the brooks with each hand-scoop of fresh clear water as he slaked his thirst, digesting the news of the outdoors with every mouthful of tongue-biting dill-seed. . . .

Gazing upward at Brushy Mountain, Crustabread tried to locate the particular spot where the grassy ledge had been. It was a ledge inhabited since the beginnings of Minnipin knowledge by the giant wosso birds, who came each spring to lay their eggs and raise their brood. And each spring a

Crustabread visited the big untidy nest and exchanged all but two of the eggs for smooth stones. Roasted wosso eggs were a great delicacy.

But three springs ago the wosso birds had forsaken the ledge. They must have recognized the danger, unlike Crustabread's parents, who had clambered eagerly up to the ledge to claim the spring yield of eggs, only to fall like stick-dolls a few moments later as the great grassy ledge broke away from the mountain and hurtled down, narrowly missing Crustabread himself, who saw the whole thing.

Already the scene was dimming in his memory, like the scar on the mountain, which had turned from stark white to only a lighter blotch on the stone face. One day he would come here and be unable to find the exact spot.

Turning away at last, he began to eat the dried reed-cakes he had brought in his pocket, washing down the crumbs with the clear water of the stream. The day stretched out before him. He could search for honey trees or climb the new trail he had started hacking out on the side of Brushy Mountain last season, or he could try to mark out with his eye a path to the wosso birds' new nest high up the mountain. Even now he heard the shrill hunting scream of the mother bird as she wheeled the sky above the trees.

But strangely, nothing appealed to him. Instead, he felt drawn toward home and the village. An odd sense of unease had taken hold of him. Perhaps it was the penetrating damp of the woods, for though the sun was blazing, here under the thick-laced branches the very air was sodden.

He made a half-hearted attempt to look for honey trees and then gave in to his feelings and started back toward the village. It was midday.

Long before he reached the edge of the woods, he knew that something was wrong. It was in the cry of the tattle-birds and the number of woodmice darting, wheeling about the forest floor, the coming and going of the scampers, the excited chitterings of the stripers. And underlying all the noise of the woods was the changed sound of Water Gap itself. The echo wasn't right.

Hurrying his steps, he finally came to the last of the trees and mounted, with some trepidation, the little rise that stood between him and the sarcen field. At the top he stopped short.

Before him lay a lake. It stretched from his feet across the valley as far as he could see, and on his left it stretched all the way to Frostbite. Where the river had been, there was only a line of turbulence in the great swirl of muddy water, and beyond this line, riding the ripples like crazy, clumsy boats, were the cottages of Water Gap. They weren't really floating, Crustabread realized after a moment's staring. It was only the motion of the flood.

And his own house . . . ? If it still stood, fish were swimming in and out the windows. Not a reed of its thatch showed above the sullen flood.

A brooding quiet hung over the great expanse of water, but at his feet it lapped and slurped and nibbled the soaked ground.

Suddenly he began to run. He fled up the valley, along the rim of flooded ground. The lake was narrowing now, and as Crustabread's course changed toward the riverbed, chimes were borne faintly on the breeze up the valley. . . .

Hear the whisper, whisper, whisper,
That lost and far off whisper,
And remember, member, member,
The whisper of Glocken's bell. . . .

There were still folk in the village!

The peal of bells changed its lugubrious tone to one of light-heart.

Silver chimes, oh silver chimes,
Ring out for all the silver times. . . .

What did it all mean? Had the flood happened so fast that they couldn't get out? His head was all kim-kam, like the happenings of the day. Even the flood was happening backward, for the farther upsteam he went, the smaller the flood circle. The edge of the water was now leading him back to the river bank; he could see a line of willows that must mark the Watercress. He would rest his bursting lungs there before going on to Deep-as-a-Well for help. . . .

He barely made it to the first willow before his legs gave out, and he slumped to the ground. An instant later he jerked his head up. Above the pounding of his heart and the wash of the river, he had heard another sound.

"Craven!" It was a shrill accusing voice. "Glocken is still in the tower, and I won't go another ear's length without him!"

"But Silky," and this voice had oiled tears in it, "we left the little raft for him. And he promised to come right along."

"Mincewit!" Silky sounded so fierce that Crustabread pressed closer to the ground. "You know what Glocken is. He'll start thinking he's a great hero playing the carillon while everybody else gets away, and then it will suddenly be too late, and he'll not get out— Oh Scumble, how can you be so spineless!"

Crustabread had no more intention of getting into this dispute than he would have of interrupting a mother wosso bird feeding on a woodmouse. On the other hand, he was becoming extremely damp. And Glocken. . . . He frowned, uncertain. Didn't the foolish one know that the tower could dissolve beneath him—that dried river clay under water becomes wet river clay once more?

The chimes continued their gay peal:

Silver chimes, oh silver chimes,
In olden lands and golden climes. . . .

Crustabread's left hand felt suddenly wet. Lifting it, he stared as the imprint left in the earth slowly filled with water. In the short time he had lain there, the flood had crept up until it was but half a lap away!

"But it may be that not everybody *is* out of the village," Scumble was protesting feebly. "That's why Glocken is waiting. We didn't *count* the folk going by."

"You saw the Mayor in the last boat," said Silky. "If he left Water Gap, that means everybody else did. Except Glocken!"

Crustabread decided that there was no choice. With a sigh he gathered himself up from the soggy ground and squelched through the trees to the edge of the angry river. It was bank-full, a turbulent brown road through the country-side. Scumble and Silky were having their confab in a small craft, which was toed in on the bank as though it had run aground. He was clinging mightily to a slender birch that grew out of the water, while she dug her paddle angrily into the water every now and then.

Crustabread hailed them and hailed them again before they left off their glaring at each other to glance his way.

"Heigh!" His voice sounded ridiculously loud, and he gulped with embarrassment. "Ng . . . the water is coming up. I'll go with you to fetch Glocken."

If Silky was surprised to see him, she gave no more sign of it than if they had met in the market square on one of Crustabread's trips to the village. "Then be quick," she commanded. "We'll leave this . . . this JELLY on the bank." She raked Scumble with scornful eyes. "The smell of fish is getting too much for me anyway."

Scumble abjectly swallowed her barb. "I didn't say I *wouldn't* go," he pleaded. "I just said it was unwise. I was afraid for *you!*"

"I don't need any help being afraid," snapped Silky. "Start paddling if you're going to take up space. Crusta-bread, you can use this one."

Crustabread took the paddle from her without question. It was a long time since anybody had told him what to do, and oddly enough it was rather comforting not to make deci-sions.

So began the journey down the roiling, boiling Water-cress. The craft rocked and bumped and sometimes turned completely around before they gained control of it.

"We'll never make it," Scumble gasped out after they had narrowly escaped foundering on a submerged something.

"Don't talk so much!" Silky's voice was fierce. "Just paddle!"

The carillon played on, echoing across the sea of water in eerie quavers. Glocken had gone back to the haunting

> *Hear the whisper, whisper, whisper,*
> *That lost and far off whisper,*
> *And remember, member, member,*
> *The whisper of Glocken's bell. . . .*

Around them rose well-known landmarks, made unfamiliar now in their liquid setting. The great emily tree that marked the first bend of the river from the village stood aloof and unfriendly in a watery landscape, and the houses in the village beyond were small unfamiliar blocks thrown down helter-skelter in the water.

"It's very odd," Silky said suddenly. "All the cottages are there, but it doesn't look like Water Gap at all. It doesn't even look like any village."

"Ng . . ." It was hard to get your voice started when you weren't used to talking. Crustabread took another gulp to oil the voiceway. "Ng . . . the pattern is gone. You don't see things by themselves. Only in patterns."

Silky looked at him as though she had never seen *him* outside a pattern, but she only said, "Why do you make that funny sound when you talk?" and turned her attention to the cottages they were approaching. Water lapped at the windows, and inside they could dimly make out the shapes of furniture bobbing about. As they passed the corner of one house, a piece of clay as big as Crustabread's head thunked into the water.

Dodging the debris that darted at them and swung away, nibble-nabble, they made their way between the half-immersed houses until they finally shot out into the square. The top chamber in the bell tower stood well above the flood, but the first flight of steps was covered, and the boat bumped gently against a window in the second flight as they came to rest.

"Holloa!" called Scumble. "Holloa, Glocken! Come down!"

The chimes ceased, leaving a long drawn-out echo behind. Glocken's head appeared through one of the window slits in the tower above them.

"Glocken, come down at once!" ordered Silky. "The water is still rising."

"Can't," replied Glocken. "I'm waiting for Gam Lutie."

Gam Lutie! They stared at each other in consternation. Gam Lutie still in the village!

"Where is the raft?" Silky called up to the window.

"Gam Lutie. She went to get the treasures." Glocken leaned out farther, his fair hair flopping over his eyes. "It's really quite a flood, isn't it?"

"Glocken," said Silky, "you must come down this instant. It's dangerous!"

"You get used to the idea after a while," he said, shrugging. "And Gam Lutie thinks we'll be all ri—" His eyes suddenly widened as he looked beyond their heads. The others turned in time to see Goober's frail old cottage slide into the water. One moment it was there, and the next it was not.

Glocken's head disappeared from the slit, and they heard the plat-plat-plat of his feet on the stairs. The water was lapping over the window ledge.

A moment later he appeared, a bulging pouch slung over one shoulder, in his hand a flat something, which he carefully stowed in his heart pocket before stepping into the boat. He gave a regretful look back at the tower as they finally pulled away. "I would have liked to save my bells. . . ."

They set off for Gam Lutie's house, but once out of the square, they promptly lost their way amongst the bewildering welter of roofs and chimneys. Baffled, Crustabread stopped paddling.

"Straight ahead," said Scumble. "I think."

"To the right," said Silky. "I'm sure."

"Gam Lutie's house," Glocken intervened, "has the biggest chimney in Water Gap and lies to the left, three roofs past the scalloped thatch of Nail the Carpenter, turn right at the chimney-with-the-stone-missing-in-the-middle, count three chimneys more, veer to the left, and it's the roof just beyond the ragged thatch of old Warp's place."

Crustabread gaped at him.

Silky's laughter spun into the air. "Oh, Glocken, I'll never tease you about dreaming in your bell tower again!"

A woven mat sailed past like a miniature raft and wrecked itself against a floating basket of winter onions. Part of a bed frame idled against the chimney-with-the-stone-missing-in-the-middle. A half-submerged door, its knocker still bright with polishing, appeared beside their boat, then slid along its way in sinister silence.

Gam Lutie's house was on the highest point of Water

Gap, and though it was now surrounded by water, the flood had risen only shin-deep inside. The reason for her delay in leaving was immediately apparent. The raft stood by the open door so heavily laden with the ancient bronze chests of treasure that it was stuck fast in the mud.

Gam Lutie, spattered with muddy water from nose to toes, wasted no time on greetings. "You'll have to put some of these chests in the boat. The raft refuses to budge." Gam Lutie's stern features might have become obscured by her disheveled state, but her voice had lost none of its command. "In any case, the raft is too dangerous. We might lose some of the treasures."

"But will there be room in the boat?" Glocken protested feebly.

"Scumble can ride on the raft," said Gam Lutie. "He won't mind."

Scumble's eyes opened as wide as they would go. "But . . . but what if you lost *me?*" he squawked.

"Nonsense," said Gam Lutie. "You can hang on. The treasure has no arms."

Crustabread had never seen the dread descendant of Gammage's sister so near-at-hand before and caught himself gaping. He cast an inquiring look at Glocken and Silky, but neither of them looked like disputing Gam Lutie's command. Despair on his face, Scumble meekly rose to do Gam Lutie's bidding.

"Ng. . . ." For a moment Crustabread could not even locate his voice, but once he got hold of it, it was far from a squeak. "Scumble, sit down. We'll take that smallest chest into the boat. If the raft still won't move, we'll offload chests until it does. We'll need some rope, Gam Lutie, for towing the raft. Glocken, help me get that little chest on board." Oblivious to Gam Lutie's frozen face, he used the paddle to work the boat up next to the raft.

"In Water Gap," said Gam Lutie in chips of ice, "I am the one who decides what we do."

Crustabread didn't spare her a glance. "Today only the flood orders." He reached out for one end of the smallest coffer, while Glocken leaned over to grasp the other end. "And the flood . . . ease it forward, Glocken . . . is impatient. The rope, Gam Lutie."

She still stood there agape, but when the raft, lightened of its load, gave a little bob, she turned and sloshed back into her house to fetch the rope.

3

The best honey is often stored in ordinary crocks.

—Muggles, *Further Maxims*

As they threaded their way between the houses, towing the heavy raft, they found sudden gaps in the orderly rows. Thatched roofs hovered on the water over their collapsed frames or floated off by themselves. Glocken looked back one last time as they came abreast of the emily tree. His tower still stood proud above the water. He patted his heart pocket and was reassured by the flat hard shape of the Whisper Stone, which at the last moment he had snatched from its niche. Worthless it might be, but it was as much a part of him as his name. He liked to remember hearing his father say, "If the first Glocken had spent less time scratching on a stone and more time coming through the river tunnel, he might not have perished in the flood."

They passed the emily tree and began the battle upstream. The raft swung clumsily behind them, snagging against trees and high-growing bushes and having to be worked free. Twice they went aground. And always the flood outran them.

"They'll take us in at Deep-as-a-Well," Scumble said, as they rested for a moment on their paddles.

Deep-as-a-Well! Glocken's heart gave a bounce. He was

going to see it at last . . . a village plunked down in a round green valley like a cooking pot, a toy village such as Carver fashioned for children. And the folk—what sort of folk *would* live in a grass-green cooking pot? Impatiently, he seized his paddle and dipped deep into the flood.

But when they finally came out from the screen of trees, he stared at first with disbelief and then with outrage. Except for a sharp rise beyond the houses, Deep-as-a-Well sprawled flat out before them and was absolutely ordinary. Why, looking out of the bell tower in Deep-as-a-Well wouldn't be any different from looking out on Water Gap. Not as exciting! For there was no Frostbite Mountain or river tunnel at hand. And—shocked, he scanned the rooftops again—for that matter, there wasn't even a bell tower!

"The water is there, too." Scumble's voice had a croak in it, as though so much water had washed out the oil.

The flood swirled around the cottages, lapping at walls with a thousand greedy tongues, savoring the taste of clay. At this rate, Glocken thought spitefully, the village would be deep as a well in no time.

Their course brought them to the market place, in the center of which stood a great post, as in any proper village square. Round the four sides the houses waited, empty and dismal, window-deep in murky water.

"There goes somebody's fine cloak," said Silky wistfully.

"And look at the soup tureen!" Scumble pointed.

A big shallow pot sailed slowly up to them, turning round and round, its contents sloshing about the sides.

Glocken's eyes lit up. "Food!" He reached out to bring in the tureen, but Crustabread, with a quick thrust of his own arm, knocked the pot out of reach.

"Never take dinner from the flood's lips."

"But . . . it's just somebody's soup he didn't get to eat. I think it's turtle done in brown berries, too. . . ."

"Watch."

A cross current had caught the tureen and sent it rocking violently. Brown flood water slurped over the brim and ran down inside to mingle with turtle and brown berry. Glocken felt a little ill.

"I'm so hungry," Silky moaned. "And my hands are all blisters." She opened both hands to show them, and the paddle, released from her clutch, plopped into the water.

"See what you've done!" Gam Lutie cried. "That's careless and wicked!"

"Oh-h-h-h," wailed Silky. She reached far out and got hold of the paddle.

Crustabread gave a yell, and at the same moment Glocken saw the submerged log, but it was too late. Like some fearful underwater monster, the log hit their boat head-on with a heavy thunk! and the boat, already out of balance from Silky's leaning over it, gave a great lurch that spilled Minnipins in all directions.

When Glocken surfaced, gasping and snorting and choking, he looked round wildly for something to catch hold of. The post! The market-place post! If he could just reach it! He flung himself toward it, went under, came up, floundered, and might have been sucked down once more and for all time had a wave not flung him against the post, where he clung like a wet cloth blown against a tree. He felt mostly dead.

Then Scumble burst out of the water half an arm's length away, spouting like a giant blowfish. From somewhere Glocken summoned the strength to reach out a hand and tow him to the post. Blinking to clear his stinging eyes, he looked frantically round for signs of the others. But there was only the boat, rocking gently and emptily in the flood, and the raft nudging it. A sick feeling began to grow in the pit of him. Even if they did bob to the surface, what could he do to save them? Unless they came up within reaching distance . . .

Once, long ago, someone in Water Gap said that children should be taught to swim, but folk had argued against the idea—the current was too fast, they said, and the children might be swept through the tunnel, past all saving. Besides, and this was the most telling point, since no Water Gapian could swim, how could anybody teach anybody else?

Water churned behind him, and Glocken felt his heart leap. But when, carefully hugging the post and Scumble, he swung round to look, there were only spreading ripples. Something big and dark, like a monstrous frog, went skating past him underwater.

"Did . . . did you see that?" he whispered, and Scumble's bugged-out eyes were answer enough.

Now there was a splash hard by the empty boat. The great brownish frog swelled up above the water, went down again with a sort of sucking sound, and then reappeared, dragging with it a sodden form. Glocken's mouth dropped open. It was . . . the form was Silky!

He gave a cry, but the brown frog, after heaving Silky over the side of the boat, billowed back into the water.

"It's Crustabread!" Scumble gasped. "That's Crustabread! He's SWIMMING!"

Glocken watched in dumb amazement while the froglike Crustabread hauled Gam Lutie dripping out of the water and draped her over the side of the boat next to Silky. A moment later the boat swung slowly toward the post, the towed raft yawing to one side.

In a daze Glocken somehow got himself and Scumble aboard. Nail the Carpenter was pounding wood pegs inside his chest, and he slumped down in the boat to wait for him to finish. He closed his eyes to shut out the sight of Silky and Gam Lutie, still hanging over the side of the boat like cloth dolls fished from the washtub, limp and bloodless and without life. Water dribbled from their mouths.

"Here," said Scumble, hoarse from swallowing flood water. "Give me a hand."

Glocken couldn't move, but he did. On his knees he helped Scumble haul Silky and Gam Lutie the rest of the way into the boat, though there seemed little point. He shut his eyes again. Perhaps if he didn't look at them, their drowning wouldn't be true. . . .

"Face up and tilted back. Make the windpipe straight," said Scumble, "and do what I do. But first make sure she is not eating her tongue."

What was he jabbering about? Glocken pulled himself up, opened his eyes . . .

Scumble must have suddenly gone mad. Incredibly, he pinched Gam Lutie's nose shut (*Gam Lutie*'s nose!) and clapped his mouth over her mouth and blew!

36

Glocken could only stare. And then as he saw Gam Lutie's chest rise with breathing, he understood.

He forgot his exhaustion, the hammering of Nail the Carpenter. Carefully he straightened Silky's body along the boat's side bench, letting her head hang over the end, to rest on the bronze coffer of treasure still miraculously clinging to the floor boards. Then he took a deep breath.

For a long time nothing happened. He filled Silky's lungs with his breath and waited for them to empty, charged them again, waited, charged, waited. . . . From the other side bench, where Scumble worked over Gam Lutie, came a groan, but he didn't look round. Fill. Empty. Fill. Empty.

Silky gave a shudder and then a gasp of returning life. Breath succeeded breath, steadier and stronger. Color came back into her face, and her eyelids fluttered. Glocken sank back on his heels, dizzy with relief.

Gradually he became aware that the boat had been moving for some time. Looking up, he saw that Crustabread was aboard and wielding a paddle with long, sure strokes. They had left the market place behind and were already approaching the farther limits of Deep-as-a-Well. And there, beyond the last of the houses, where the land rose abruptly and the Watercress cut deep through the hill, was the edge of the flood!

"Mind, there!" Scumble shouted, and Glocken flung himself against Silky's bench to brace himself—for he knew not what.

But it was Gam Lutie causing the commotion. Bolt upright, eyes blazing, she pointed toward the fast-receding market place.

"You don't dare," she grated out. "You DON'T DARE!"

37

But Crustabread didn't lose a stroke. Glocken, tossing his head to shake the hair out of his eyes, saw how it was that one body alone could now paddle the boat so swiftly. Behind them in the market place, tied snugly to the post, was the raft containing the precious treasure chests brought from Gam Lutie's house.

Before they entered the main course of the Watercress, Glocken and Scumble relieved Crustabread at the paddles. It took all their strength to force the boat upstream, for the crazy currents flung their craft every which way. Glocken's hands, rubbed raw from the paddle, were numb blobs at the end of his wrists. He was so cold that he had stopped shivering. But most alarming of all, he kept sinking into a doze and had to jerk himself awake before he let go of the paddle. Where was that next village . . . ? Deep-as-a-Well. . . . No, they had come through Deep-as-a-Well. What was the matter with him! The next village would be . . . would be. . . . He wagged his head to start his brain moving again. The next village. . . . He gave such a start that the boat wallowed.

"Do be careful!" Gam Lutie said crossly.

But Glocken scarcely heard. The next village was—Slipper-on-the-Water! He was going to see—he was actually going to be *in* Slipper-on-the-Water! He would see—he might even *speak* to—Walter the Earl. And Muggles. And Mingy. Curley Green and Gummy. His head suddenly felt light, as though it might float off his shoulders.

"You've stopped paddling," Silky nagged. "We've been standing still for minutes."

Glocken thrust his paddle deep into the water. The boat shot forward.

A weary time later they rounded the final bend, and before them lay Slipper-on-the-Water. It swarmed with life. There were gathered on the bank more folk than Glocken had ever seen together at one time. Huddled forms sat or lay on the ground, and flying about amongst them were cloaks gay as flitter-wings. These, then, were the folk of Slipper-on-the-Water who, as a token of their esteem for the Outlaw-Heroes, had forsaken the time-honored Watercress green.

A stout Slipperian in a blue cloak pulled them in close to the dock with a pole hook, and eager hands helped them from the boat. They were passed to other supporting arms and shoulders, which conveyed them to a grassy plot and found spots for them to sink down onto the ground. There they became just five more sodden folk amongst all the other water-logged scatterlings. A strong smell of drying fish hung about them.

In the middle of the crowded space a great pot steamed over a cooking fire, wafting so many mouth-watering scents that Glocken couldn't sort them out. There were turtle and fish mingled with sustaining milk-root, winter cabbage and wild onion, garlic and watercress, the heady blood-bark and dark tang of huddlestone tansy. It was like the smells of fifty soup pots from fifty kitchens all mingled together. Come to that, Glocken suddenly thought, it probably was. As the first flooded-out scatterlings landed at their village, goodwives would have come running with their hot soups snatched up from their stoves—it was the law of hospitality. And now all the soups steamed and bubbled together. . . .

Glocken licked his lips and shut his eyes for a moment to enjoy the smell better. A moment later he opened them on a queer little smiling fellow in an even queerer high conical hat, who was offering steaming cups to the shivering flood victims.

"Eat it up and suck it down," he said in a sort of chant, "or, if you prefer,

> "Eat it down,
> Suck it up.
> Whistle twice
> For a second cup."

He delivered cups into their hands, winked, doffed his yellow hat in a deep bow that almost put his nose into Glocken's soup, and seemed about to deliver himself of a second verse when there was a sudden call of "Soup needed! Soup wanted here!" He clapped his hat back on his head at a ridiculous angle and took off for the soup pot, his yellow cloak flouncing over downcast heads.

Then a rather fat, untidy Slipperian, her middle tied up with a spotted orange sash like a sack of reed flour, stopped in front of Glocken and his four companions and gave each of them a searching look. She dropped to her knees beside Glocken and opened a basket that she carried. From it she took a clay bottle, which she first shook and then poured from onto a small cloth. This she slapped against Glocken's cheek, and suddenly the whole side of his face caught fire.

He jerked back, but the orange sash seemed prepared for that. "It stings now," she soothed him, "but that means it won't hurt later." With her other hand she brushed his hair back off his forehead. "There, isn't that better?"

Glocken glared at her.

"Here," she said anxiously, "have a pepmint, do," and she pulled a crumpled bag of pepmints from the pocket of her untidy dress.

Glocken turned his head away from the sorry-looking sweet with disdain. "No, thank you," he said.

But Silky spoke up quickly. "Oh, please may I have one?" Orange-Sash pushed her miserable pepmint drops round, and they all sat sucking on them like so many sarcen-flies.

Somewhere, surely somewhere, in this bustle of rainbow cloaks were the five famous Outlaw-Heroes of Slipper-on-the-Water! There were any number of distinguished-looking villagers flying importantly about, but the only folk who approached their huddled little party were the odd-bodies. Here came two more of them. One was tall and seedy-looking, with a pronounced nose and a threadbare cloak which had seen better days, but those days had been far off and long ago. His hat had a tatty feather sticking in it. The other had a face like an angry nutcracker. Under one arm he carried a tool box or chest, which he patted nervously from time to time.

The tall seedy one with the nose pointed an ashplant staff at them. "All taken care of?" he asked.

"Oh yes, that we are," said Scumble. "Could do with a bit more soup if there's enough to go round?"

Tool-Box hurried off to the soup pot, and in less than a minute fresh bowls of soup were warming their hands and stomachs, brought this time by a Slipperian with floating pale hair like milkweed bursting from a pod.

Glocken's heart lurched. Pale hair floating. . . . The Curley Green in Walter the Earl's *Glorious True Facts* was said to have gossamer hair! Could this creature by the remotest chance be . . . ? No, it couldn't. Decidedly not. Curley Green was a flame shining in the night, a silver streak in bluest water, a chime of bells on summer air, a crystal dewdrop in the morning sun. And this creature—was a simple villager of Slipper-on-the-Water who could carry soup without putting her thumb in it but hadn't remembered to comb her hair.

He felt suddenly peevish. Days and weeks and months had gone into his dreams of one day visiting Slipper-on-the-Water, and now that after untold difficulties, sodden, half-starved, bone-weary, he had at last reached the home of heroes, look what he found—a succession of feeble-witted villagers, no more heroic than Stonebreaker the Mason or Belch the Bottle-Maker, for all their colored cloaks.

And then quite suddenly he ceased to fume. The warm soup had reached its mark, and the long day had caught up with him so that between one thought and the next, he slid into sleep.

Later, he felt himself lifted to his feet, and somehow he bent his knees and flapped his feet along cobblestones, until he was led through a doorway and allowed to sink into a cloud of softness. Hands fussed at him, removed his soggy garments, and replaced them with a downy sleeping shirt that smelled of verbena. Sleep closed down again and held him fast until a morning ray of sunlight poked at his eyelids. He opened them the merest slit.

"He's waking up now," a voice growled.

"Good. I'll put the flopcakes on." This voice sounded familiar, and Glocken opened one eye wider to be sure. It was Orange-Sash, all right, even more untidy than yesterday—as though she had slept in her clothes. The growly voiced one was old Tool-Box.

He let his eyes rove over the room. There were piles of things. Yes, piles. Heaps of all manner of objects everywhere on the floor. In the corner, under the table, near the fireplace, yes, heaps. Glocken suddenly wondered if all the people of Slipper-on-the-Water were like those he had met so far. If so, no wonder the Outlaw-Heroes had left the village to go live on the Knoll!

He craned his neck to look further about the room for signs of Silky . . . Gam Lutie. . . . What had become of the others?

"Where are my friends?" he demanded.

The grouchy one pointed. Glocken, turning his head, saw stretched out on comforters on the floor and still asleep, Scumble and Crustabread. Well, he thought, at least that explained two of the heaps!

"And Silky? And Gam Lutie?"

"Across the market place," said Orange-Sash. "Come, sit and eat. To honor you, I have put the last of the honey into the flopcakes."

Glocken climbed willingly out of the welter of comforters and found himself clothed in a well-patched green sleeping shirt. Skirting one of the heaps near his bed, he sat down to the table, and then, suddenly remembering, he clapped his hand to his breast. The Whisper Stone!

"I put it safely away," Orange-Sash said, nodding toward the heap in the far corner. "I thought it must be precious."

"And the scrolls?" asked Glocken. "In the pouch?"

"Oh yes," said Orange-Sash. "Same heap. The thin bossy one with you tried to say they were really hers to look after, but we told her she could settle with you afterwards."

Glocken felt his jaw drop. This untidy creature and her rock-faced spouse might have mince for wits, but they had stout backbones. Ordinary folk didn't hold out from Gam Lutie.

Glocken hurled himself on to the flopcakes and made quick work of them, but Orange-Sash brought more and more until he was filled. Then Crustabread and Scumble woke up and were fed. All the time that they ate, the grumbly Tool-Box groused and growled, but Orange-Sash never lost her good humor. Indeed, she appeared to enjoy the grousings. After a while he went out to learn the condition of the river. He took his tool chest with him.

Glocken was just considering the tempting warmth of the bed when there came a tap at the door. Silky and Gam Lutie walked in, followed by the blown milkweed hair, the yellow conical hat, and finally the threadbare cloak swinging an ashplant.

For a time the room was full of chatter, until the seedy one thumped on the floor with his ashplant. "If it please you, I should like to establish Facts. Will the one called Scumble please to answer the questions I have to put." He swung the ashplant up to point at the sluice-gate keeper's chest but without waiting for agreement plunged into his questions.

When had they first noted the flood? Had the river been badly swollen from the rains? What of the tunnel? Did the water come *from* the tunnel? Had the tunnel ever become blocked with debris? Could it be blocked now, perhaps, by the litter from the swollen river? Or could there have been a fall of rock inside the mountain? Or . . . ?

To Glocken's surprise, Scumble had noticed all sorts of things that no one else had. Yes, the water had certainly backed in from the tunnel. The heavy rains had only hurried the flooding—they had not caused it. As for flood litter or a rock fall. . . . Scumble shrugged. It had never happened before, but who was to know . . . ? Yes, the tunnel when last seen was mouth-full.

The seedy one fell to pinching his long nose in silent thought, and the rest watched him think, until the door was flung open and the grouchy one stomped in, tools rattling in his box. "Water still up," he grated. "To the brim. No higher. No lower."

"I see." Abandoning his nose, the seedy one turned to Glocken. "I understand that you have some sort of map of the outside—of the other side of Frostbite."

Glocken gaped at him. "Me? Map?"

"A stone then, with scratchings on it," the other said impatiently. "I must see it."

Glocken turned accusingly to Orange-Sash.

"It was a breach of hospitality," Orange-Sash confessed, "but the urgent situation perhaps excuses me for mentioning. . . ."

"Really!" Gam Lutie spoke up for the first time. "You seem to be taking a great deal upon yourselves."

Orange-Sash turned pink to the roots of her sketchily brushed hair. "Yes, I know," she admitted humbly. "I apologize."

"Map . . ." Glocken said wonderingly. "Do you mean that the Whisper Stone is a *map?*"

The seedy one snorted with exasperation. "Do *you* mean that you never noticed that it's Frostbite Mountain backward? Now tell us about the Whisper. I know of it only by name, but the ancient manuscripts hint of some extraordinary power. What is it? Where is it?"

The milkweed hair spoke up in a voice like a chime. "We don't want to pry into your secrets, so please don't be angry with us. But don't you see—we can't let you go off outside the valley without putting together every scrap of knowledge that we have. It is a perilous journey, and we must help you in any way we can."

Glocken almost jumped out of the verbena-scented nightshirt. "Go outside!" he croaked. "What do you mean? We have no intention of going outside the valley."

"Oh." The five Slipperians glanced knowingly at each other. The one in the conical hat looked at the ceiling beams and whistled softly to himself.

"Ng . . . why should we go outside?" asked Crustabread finally.

"Why"—Orange-Sash faltered—"to take the stopper out of the tunnel, of course. We understand why you want to keep the journey a secret, but we promise not to tell folk and alarm them—"

"Stopper?" Scumble's voice slid up in a squeal.

"Why yes," said Orange-Sash, "or whatever it is that is making the Watercress flow back on itself instead of going out of the valley through the tunnel."

"And then the map," spoke up the milkweed one. "Walter the Earl says—"

"The map puzzles me," interrupted the seedy one. "Are we to believe that this Whisper bell was deliberately left outside the valley? Why? Or could it be that . . . ?"

But Glocken wasn't listening. "Walter the Earl?" he

cried. "Walter the Earl has seen my stone? When can I see *him*? And the others—Muggles and Mingy. Gummy. Curley Green. The great Heroes! And you say Walter the Earl has seen my stone? Did *he* think it was a map?"

The five Slipperians stared at him open-mouthed, as though they thought his brain had turned to mince. And then the one in the peculiar conical hat suddenly grinned.

"You never know," he said gleefully, "when you see a frame, what goes on inside, or what's its name." He took off the ridiculous hat and swept the floor with it in a gigantic bow. "My dear young bell-ringer, nothing could be easier! In fact, you are wearing, if I am not mistaken, a Hero's nightshirt this very moment."

Glocken felt as though a bell had suddenly been struck inside his head.

"May I have the pleasure of introducing"—the conical hat proceeded, and he flourished his sun-yellow cloak to include the other four Slipperians—"us!"

A whole carillon went off in Glocken's head.

"You!" he choked, and his eyes traveled from the orange sash that was tied round Muggles' middle to the tool chest—no, money box!—in Mingy's clasp, took in Curley Green's milkweed hair and Gummy's sun-cloak and yellow conical hat and finally let his new-sighted eyes dwell on the threadbare, long-nosed Walter the Earl.

"At your service," said Walter the Earl briskly, delivering a precise bow. "And now allow us the great honor of assisting the five New Heroes to make plans for their perilous journey into the outside world."

4

Some words cannot be spoken, no matter how the tongue pushes at the teeth.

—Muggles, *Further Maxims*

Twenty times that day, and the next, and the next, and then one more, Glocken wanted to cry out, "No, no, no, it's all a shocking mistake!" But once past that first stunning moment when the Heroes of Slipper-on-the-Water took it for granted that the five Water Gapians were heroes-in-the-budding, it grew harder and harder to deny. With each passing hour it became more certain that the five Water Gapians were destined to be heroes in spite of themselves.

In vain Glocken had pointed out that first day that the logical folk to go adventuring were those who already had been away from home, who had had experience of a separate existence from the village. Walter the Earl had been as obtuse as his famous ancestor by that name. "It is generous of you to offer a share in your adventure. You have a true hero's heart. But we will not steal any of your glory from you, though we stand ready to help should you need us."

"You can't give away your own adventure," agreed Muggles. "It is a part of you, and if you do not play it out, it will never come true for anyone."

I don't *want* to play it out, Glocken shouted inside his head, but how could he bring the shameful words to his lips

48

when he had been called a hero? A hero . . . ! Heroes were woven of a superior fabric. Heroes went forward without question and with unafraid hearts and a pulse that sounded thu-*rum*, thu-*rum*, not pittle-pittle-*phut*.

While Glocken and the other Water Gapians looked at each other stupefied, Walter the Earl knelt by Muggles' hearth and with a hunk of chalkstone sketched a map of the valley. He put three crosses on it. One marked Slipper-on-the-Water; another, the tunnel which led through the Sunset Mountains to the outside world; and the third on the other side of Frostbite, where the Watercress must empty from the tunnel.

"Three days' journey each way," Crustabread suddenly said into the silence when the chalkstone had stopped squeaking. "Ng . . . we should each pack food for seven or eight days, in case of . . . in case. Water, too. And good heavy cloaks. The nights will be cold."

"Really, Crustabread," said Gam Lutie. "Your brain must be failing. You certainly don't expect me to go. I have duties here."

"But of course," said Silky unexpectedly. "Don't you see? It arranged itself. It was fated the moment we went back in the boat to get you and Glocken, and Glocken took the Whisper Stone out of the wall and brought it along for Walter the Earl to see and—and—why, it's even fate that there are five of us—just like the Old Heroes!"

Fated, Glocken thought glumly on that first day. *Fated*, he thought glumly three days later, as he tried to shift his pack to ease his aching back. The hot sun was like an explosion on his head, and the way along the Little Trickle was treacherous, for the heavy rains had slicked the path. The

49

others straggled ahead of him like unsteady beetles, except for Crustabread, whose movements were always neat. They must be getting close to the Knoll now, where the Old Heroes were awaiting them—the Knoll where the famous battle with the Mushrooms had taken place.

The whole affair was ridiculous. Take the way they had left the village. You might say that they had sneaked out, like so many deserters, instead of marching out like heroes to a fanfare of music and a wild clamor of bells—come to that, Slipper-on-the-Water didn't even possess a bell. The quiet departure had been the idea of that Muggles.

"Better not to alarm the village and perhaps cause panic," she had said in her hesitant manner. "They might try to stop you, and you wouldn't want that. . . ."

Wouldn't I, thought Glocken.

"If the Council of Periods begin to talk about it," Mingy rumbled, "they'll still be talking as the water fills their mouths."

"We can go ahead of you to the Knoll," Muggles went on. "We would do that anyway, to make more room in the village for the scatterlings. We'll pretend we're getting the houses there ready to take you five in with us. Nobody will have the least idea that you've left the valley."

"Of course we'll escort you through the old gold mine and see you on your way from there," said Walter the Earl.

"Isn't it exciting!" cried Curley Green.

Glocken felt ill.

But the plans and plottings had gone on, and everything was accomplished in just about the fashion you would expect of somebody who kept the household goods in heaps on the floor. Everybody kept interrupting everybody else, and that least-dependable-of-all, Gummy, insisted on talking in rhymes. Glocken still felt outraged over

> *The chap called Glocken*
> *Sets the bell tower rockin'*
> *When he thumps on his silver bells.* . . .

He would like to thump Gummy a good one.

Then there was Curley Green, who paid no attention to anybody except to draw and paint pictures of them. Glocken smarted whenever he looked at his own picture with the lock of hair strayed over one eye. She was deliberately trying to make a fool of him—as though he walked around with his hair in his face all the time!

As for Mingy, he did nothing but grumble and rattle his money box and object to everything, while Muggles smiled fecklessly at his every word when she wasn't dishing up homilies along with her spiced soups.

Walter the Earl, with his high-flown way of talking, came closest to being a genuine hero, but his shabby cloak and his terrible conceit spoiled the effect, and even his regal tones became comic when the talk ran on simple subjects.

No, these were not like the heroes of old, the great Gammage and his sister Gam Lutie. Even the first Glocken, who perished outside the valley, seemed more of a hero than these odd-bodies from Slipper-on-the-Water. So much for Walter the Earl's *Glorious True Facts*, Glocken thought with annoyance.

Wearily, he brushed his arm over his forehead where his hair clung in a damp strand and searched for some sign of the Knoll ahead, but the trees closed in, and there was only the swollen murmur of the Little Trickle and the songs of birds to break the stillness.

The sun was high in the sky when they came to a natural clearing. The ground sloped gently up from the stream, and at the top—Glocken saw smoke rising from the three stone houses on the Knoll. There was a faint shout, and then he saw small figures at the brim waving and doing some sort of wild welcoming dance. One part of him felt a surge of joy and relief at the sight, but another part sank further into gloom. They were so—so frivolous. They couldn't seem to think seriously for two minutes in a line. It was all wrong.

The feeling persisted even after they had been greeted like old friends on top of the Knoll and sat down to a glorious feast of fresh trout dressed with lemon-mint, baked seed-bread, savory milk-root, and jellied cowslip. Everybody talked at once and laughed, and the courses got muddled so that the jellied cowslip landed on top of the trout, and then everybody laughed at that too. Everybody except Gam Lutie, who was always serious—and Glocken. His scowl grew deeper.

Silky finally burst into his dark thoughts. "What's wrong with you?"

Gam Lutie answered for him, with a sniff. "It is fitting that we bear a more serious mien. We shall possibly become the saviors of the Minnipins."

The Slipperians looked at her with their eyebrows raised high, and Glocken felt annoyed all over again, but this time, strangely, with Gam Lutie.

"Gammage himself wasn't above a joke," said Walter the Earl slowly. "It is recorded that on one occasion during the long journey to this valley, he was thumped on the head with a frypan for pretending to put a lizard in the soup pot."

"I find that past believing," said Gam Lutie.

"Fact." Walter the Earl shrugged his threadbare shoulders. "It is in the Accounts. It is History. It is Fact."

Gam Lutie drew herself up to her fullest, which was very full indeed. "Gammage was a great man and a great leader," she said. "He brought our people from the Golden Mountain to this land through terrors that would stop any ordinary body. He was good and wise and just."

"He was even folk," said Walter the Earl dryly. "Like the rest of us."

Gummy, who had finished his meal, suddenly yawned and stretched out on the grass. "Don't bother to call me until the next meal," he yawned. "I am about to fall deeply asleeply."

"Wrong," said Curley Green. "It's time to start for the Sunset Mountains."

But it was an hour before they finally left the Knoll. There were stone bottles to be filled with sweet Watercress water. . . .

"It's really Little Trickle water," said Mingy.

"Same thing," Muggles answered. "Now somebody help fasten the packs on."

There was a final dispute with Gam Lutie over the small bronze chest of treasure, which she insisted had to go where she went. She had her way, of course, but somehow it fell to Scumble's lot to carry the chest. Muggles put it in a hamper for him, but Glocken felt annoyed that the oil-presser didn't at least make a protest. Sometimes it seemed that Scumble *deserved* to smell of fish oil.

There was also an argument over the swords. Walter the

Earl wanted the New Heroes to wear the armor and carry the banners as well as the heavy blackened swords of the Minnipins. For the first time Glocken's eyes lit up. This was the stuff of legend, of heroes, of history. But even he had to admit, when he had allowed himself to be buckled into the armor, that a six-day trek under a desert sky was not ideal for the wearing of a metal suit. Nor could it be carried on their backs, for possible later use, without bending them double. The swords and sword belts they accepted, though it was hard to believe that these dull blackened blades could ever shine with the radiance of the sun.

There were gifts to be presented, like the miniature scroll which Walter the Earl gave to Glocken. "You must keep a record of all that happens," he commanded. "Truly and faithfully. Set down as Fact only the things that are true."

Mingy offered up his sand cloak. "Color of rock and sand. Makes you invisible. Wore it myself against the Mushrooms." He thrust it roughly at Crustabread.

Curley Green and Gummy presented a small sheaf of birch pages strung together with vine. "Muggles' *Maxims*," Curley Green explained. "It's for when you're in real trouble. You simply open up the pages and read where your eye falls. It will give you advice."

Glocken gave a snort of derision, which he turned into a cough.

Muggles stuck an odd-looking tool, half pick, half spade, into Scumble's pack and gave Silky an herb basket to tie at her waist. Among all the other remedies was a small clay pot that contained the last of the precious ointment taken from the Mushrooms by Mingy. "Try to find the plant that gives forth this salve," she charged them. "The Mushrooms brought it from somewhere outside the valley. It is more precious than gold, for it returns life to the body."

Weary of so much advice and direction, Glocken scuffled his feet and shifted his pack on his shoulders, but Muggles had only begun her series of last advices. *If you need to eat off the land, be wary, taste delicately, swallow small. Remember that there is good in bitter, and bitter in good. Smell carefully all that you would eat. That is why your nose grows so close to your mouth. Strong smells—*"

Surely she had said all this before. Glocken could stand no more. "We know all about strong smells," he said curtly. "We've got Scumble." Shouldering his pack, he stepped off, not caring about the little astonished gasps in his wake. There was about Muggles a muddledness that irritated him beyond reason, made unkindness fly out of his mouth.

The small procession wound along the banks of the Little Trickle, with the five Old Heroes pointing out known spots to the five New Heroes. As they got nearer to the Sunset Mountains, the trees thinned and the soil became stonier. Then the trees disappeared altogether, and in a short while they were passing Mingy's Rock, where Mingy, under the protection of the invisible cloak, had lain in the hot sun waiting for the Mushrooms to emerge from the old mine in the mountain. It was big enough as rocks go, but Glocken found it disappointing. Beside his imagining of it, it was as insignificant as the invisible cloak, which had turned out not to be truly invisible at all!

They paused before the entrance to the mine to have what the Old Heroes called a picklick. But the roar of the waterfall that fed the Little Trickle was so loud that they were unable to talk without shouting. They finished lunch quickly, slung their packs on again, and without more fuss plunged into the disused gold mine. The tunnel was as black as the inside of a trout.

Walter the Earl, who was in the lead, carried a lighted candle, and the rest trailed out behind him. There was no dawdling. Glocken, who brought up the rear, looked once over his shoulder, but the wall of darkness only pressed tight against his eyeballs, and he looked back no more. When he put out his hand to steady himself, the feel of the chill damp stone walls made him shudder, and he shrank into the folds of his cloak. There was a lingering odor of mushrooms, mixed with that of burned rubbish. Glocken felt a thrill of excitement, for he suddenly realized that the mushroom smell was not that of fungus, but of the Minnipins' ancient enemy, and the burned rubbish was from the smoke screen made by Mingy when he set alight the sleeping mats and so forced the Mushrooms back into the valley.

Down, down sloped the tunnel, until it seemed they must be nearing the center of the earth. Glocken had grown used to the eerie sounds they heard as they progressed. There was the slight pad-pad of slippers on earth, the muted rustle of garments, an occasional muffled gasp as someone tripped or inadvertently touched the chill walls, the faint chink of the bronze chest Scumble carried in the basket, and a small clicking sound which puzzled him for a time until he realized that it was the chattering of his own teeth.

The tunnel leveled off finally, and the floor became more even so that they could walk a little faster, but it stretched endlessly on. The burnt smell became stronger and stronger as they advanced, and then Walter the Earl halted up ahead, and they all bumped into each other like the cars of a merry-go-long when the puller stopped too suddenly. They had entered a vast cavernous chamber.

"Been here before," said Mingy, and his voice echoed round the rough-hewn walls. "Almost smoked myself out. Don't linger on my account."

"Nor mine," said Curley Green with a shiver, and the walls echoed, *nor mine . . . nor mine . . . nor mine.*

They pressed on through other hollowed-out rooms in which the Mushrooms had dwelt, nobody knew for how long, before they entered the Land Between the Mountains.

At last the rooms gave way to another long tunnel.

"It's not far now," announced Walter the Earl from up ahead.

Glocken gave a shiver that had nothing to do with the dampness of the underground passage. Every moment was taking them farther away from what they knew, into a world where the only reality was the clicking of his own teeth. A finger of fear traced down his spine. What could they do in the great waste which Walter the Earl had described to them? They were but puny folk—not the stuff of heroes! It was ridiculous to suppose that anyone would tell of them in song and story. How could you set music to the clicking of teeth? And the penetrating fish-oil smell of Scumble—how did you put that into a hero's tale?

A flood of misery washed over him. The wasted hours he had spent in his bell tower dreaming of heroes and heroes' deeds! If he hadn't a head so stuffed with adventure, he would have brought food and clothing with him from the bell tower instead of the Whisper Stone. It was seeing the Stone had made the Old Heroes think they were headed for the outside world to take the stopper out of the Watercress tunnel. And it was his own foolish pride that had kept him from confessing the truth. . . .

With a start Glocken realized that he had fallen far behind the others. Would he ever learn not to dream! He hurried forward until he could hear the reassuring shuffle of feet and rasp of breath. Someone began to whistle—Gummy?—and then at last they all stopped. Ahead, there now appeared to be two flickering candles. Then Glocken saw that the second was a chink of light. They had reached the entrance.

Walter the Earl was inspecting the stones that he and his soldiers had used to close up this end of the tunnel against marauders five years before. They had done their work well.

"Lift out the smaller stones first," he commanded. "Then we push this biggest boulder outward like a door."

They put down their packs and set to work in the crowded confines of the tunnel. It quickly grew hot and stuffy. The sun bit at them with sharp teeth through the ever widening gaps in the door of rocks.

"That's enough," said Walter the Earl. "Mingy, Gummy. Help me move the boulder. The rest of you stay out of the way."

There was a shuffle of feet and a pause and then Walter the Earl's voice again. "One, two, three—heave! Again. One, two—" Glocken huddled by the wall and closed his eyes against the brightness of the sun. Suddenly he felt the tunnel was a good place to be. When the boulder rolled back, they would have to step into that other world. ". . . three—heave!"

The rock gave a shudder and moved a tiny bit. Smaller stones rattled down into the tunnel.

"We'll need everybody," Walter the Earl said. "Put your shoulders to it!"

And then they were all crowded together, pushing and straining against the massive stone.

One, two, three—heave! One, two, three—heave! For an eternity they strained until at last, with an agonized grating sound, the huge boulder gave way before them and swung back like a great door.

One by one they stepped out on the stony slope of the mountain into the full heat of the searing westering sun. It beat and pulsed at them, drying out the chill in their bones in an instant.

Glocken blinked and blinked his eyes to rid them of a thousand purple spots that swam before him. When at last he could see, he almost plunged back into the tunnel. A vast gray-brown waste stretched before them and to either side as far as the eye could reach. Nothing moved in the heat-shimmered air. It was a lifeless land, a place for death.

"First day's journey completed," said Walter the Earl, but his voice, which had boomed so reassuringly at them in the tunnel, sounded thin and weak in the vastness that confronted them.

5

Once upon a whisper-time—so it is told, but who would believe it?—the Glocken of Then could play the tiny golden bell to any purpose. And on a merry holiday he boasted that he could harvest a field of sarcen, and he did. But the bell would not pick up the fallen sarcen, and Glocken and the villagers worked not so merrily the rest of that holiday, and *this* I believe.

—Pretend-story, told by Glocken
to Glocken to Glocken, from
Then to Now

They stood long minutes in the wilting sunlight, staring at the end of the world. Gray-brown against gray-brown, straggles of dusty plants reared up from the face of the desert, twisted and tortured like lampreys writhing into the air. Yet there was a something, a shimmering that was like sunlight but not quite like sunlight. It was a shifting, veering motion that broke off, started up again as they stared.

Scumble tried to swallow, but his throat was suddenly as dry as the plain before them. They couldn't do it, of course. He had known all along that they would never go through with the adventure, and now. . . . Nobody could expect them to set foot in this wasteland. It was obviously and forever out of the question. In a moment Crustabread or Gam

Lutie would say it, and they could then all go back to Slipper-on-the-Water.

"Is there anything else we can do to help?" asked Walter the Earl.

The five New Heroes' heads swiveled like toys on a stick to look at him. They swiveled back to look out again upon the vast grayness. Scumble could feel his neck wiggling with the movement of his throat-knob, but he waited for someone else to speak up, to say that of course five puny Water Gapians were no match for this land lying in wait to devour them. Might as well throw five slippery trout into a sand pit and expect them to swim as to send five Minnipins into the sunstruck plain.

"Then we'll wish you good speed and hasty return," said Walter the Earl, his voice gruff.

Scumble's stomach dropped. Still no one spoke the words he knew must be said. What was the matter with them! Didn't Gam Lutie at least realize . . . ?

"We could spend the night here," said Curley Green doubtfully. "If you're . . . if you would like company."

Scumble opened his mouth, but Crustabread forestalled him.

"We're all right," he said quietly, and Scumble's stomach, hopeful for a moment, plummeted down somewhere near his knees.

But still the Slipperians lingered, to say more good-bys and deliver last bits of advice.

"It's Facts will see you through," said Walter the Earl. "Never rely on conjecture or suspicion or it-could-be."

"But if you run out of Facts," added Curley Green, "open up Muggles' *Maxims* and read what is there."

"Eat the fishcakes I packed for you tonight and tomorrow morning, but if the sun gets at them, eat no more."

"And keep your swords at hand even while you sleep. They will tell you when danger comes."

Mingy undid the money box and took from it a pouch of jingling coins. "It may be you'll find this useful. Gam Lutie, you take it in charge. Don't waste it, but use it if need be." He gave a vast sigh. "It's half the sick fund. Mind you don't lose it."

"Don't use it, don't lose it," chanted Gummy. "Just listen to it jingle, a-tingle-lingle-lingle. . . ." He began to whistle and, with a jaunty wave, strode into the tunnel. The other four Old Heroes hesitated, made as if to speak, and then, as though realizing the futility of delay, raised their arms in salute and followed Gummy's whistle.

Scumble's stomach slid from his knees on down to his ankles. He had never thought much about friends, having never had any. Folk stayed away from him—they were even careful not to jostle him in the Square, as though they were fearful of the fishy smell rubbing off on them. He was used to seeing them wince when a breeze suddenly shifted, and it hadn't bothered him—much.

But, oddly, the Old Heroes of Slipper-on-the-Water hadn't drawn back. They had accepted his fishiness like— like one of Walter the Earl's Facts. Come to think of it, they had probably *all* smelled more than a little fishy after their near-drowning in the flood. The very thought of it cheered him.

"Now then," said Gam Lutie in her rallying voice, "I suppose we might as well busy ourselves."

Scumble decided to ally himself with Crustabread, who seemed to know more what he was doing than the others, but somehow it turned out to be Glocken who went off with Crustabread along the slope to look for water. Silky and Gam Lutie settled down to examine the contents of the herb basket.

That left Scumble, as usual, alone with the smell of fish. Shrugging his aching shoulders, he wandered cautiously a little way down the slope. Odd. A moment ago there had been that shimmer, but now it was gone. The desert floor lay drear and lifeless below him. Eyes darting about in his head like skate-fish in a pond, he moved downward to take a closer look at the scraggy plants that clung to the gray-brown land. *Don't wait until you're starving to look for food.* That's what the one called Muggles had said over and over. *An empty stomach makes no footprints*, she had said. And, *It is of no use to seek milk-root in streams, nor yet watercress in a dry meadow.*

There were other advices and cautions about food:

Avoid the Nightplant both day and night.

Be wary of cherry rough and red,
Be chary of berry in gloss-green bed,
Lest you be dead, lest you be dead.

A shiver made a return trip along his backbone. The rules seemed simple enough, rattled off like that, but how was one to know about plants never before seen? *Every plant has a cousin*, Muggles had said. That might be, but if plants were like folk, there were good and bad cousins.

The first plants of any size that he reached were sown so

thickly with thorns there was no taking hold of them. Another kind, a round ball of a bush of intertwined twigs, came up abruptly in his hand, but its short root was dry and stiff. No use in that, unless it could be soaked for hours, and water, from the looks of this place, they would not find in quantity.

Then he noticed a meager plant which had pushed only a few stems out of the baked earth and he recalled another bit of advice from Muggles' lore. *What is inside the head doesn't show in the hair.* He bent over and grasped the few stray branches. But tug as he would, he couldn't pull the root from the earth. He tried to dig round the base of the plant with his fingers, but the ground was iron-hard, and his fingers only scratched at the surface. Perhaps if he tried with the spade-pick Muggles had stuck in his pack. . . .

Gam Lutie and Silky were still bent over the herb basket. "Mushroom salve, hmph!" Gam Lutie was saying, frowning at a small sealed pot. "Who ever heard of mushrooms being any good as medicine. I wouldn't put my trust in *that.*"

"It's not made *of* mushrooms," Silky explained patiently. "It's the salve that Mingy took *from* the Mushrooms—the Hairless Ones. We're supposed to try—"

"Hmph! Then why didn't she say so." Gam Lutie turned her irritation on Scumble as he came panting up to them. "We have plenty of food in our packs, and I'm sure I shan't eat anything you dig out of this sour land, if that is what you're intending to do."

"Yes, Gam Lutie." He picked up the little spade-pick and started down the slope. Again he had the feeling of movement ceasing as he moved. *It is only the sunlight shim-*

mering, he reassured himself. But a moment later he stopped dead in his tracks, and in spite of the heat, prickles of cold pulled his skin suddenly tight.

There, where he had scrabbled with his fingers round the scrawny plant, a great hole yawned at him, a hole as deep as he was high. At the bottom of the pit lay a bulbous root.

He didn't run because his legs refused to move. Straightening slowly, he let his eyes rove over the surrounding landscape, and his hand went to the hilt of the sword hanging at his side. There was nothing—nothing to be seen or—his eyes were drawn to a spot. He had caught a glimmer, a flash of brightness. It was gone now, but he kept his gaze riveted on the place. Was there a—a something crouched there, or was it only another plant, gray-brown against gray-brown? His eyeballs ached with the strain, but he didn't dare blink lest the something disappear. The hilt of the sword remained cool in his hand.

Then I am in no danger, he thought. *I should move forward as slowly as an inching worm and see.* Only, he couldn't.

Above him, on the slope, Silky called out something, and then Glocken's voice came thinly through the air. There was the sound of running feet behind him, and a moment later he felt Crustabread's grip on his arm. For just an instant he flicked his eyes away from the something, and in that instant it disappeared as completely as though it had never been there in the first place—if it had.

He answered the others' clamoring questions as best he could, pointing out the exposed root and the spot where he had seen the glimmer as though the sunlight had glanced off the staring eyes of a creature.

65

Crustabread, his sword at the ready, strode fearlessly to the spot. "Nothing here now," he called back. "Not even a plant."

"You imagined it," said Gam Lutie.

Scumble looked at the scooped-out hole. "I didn't imagine *that,*" he said slowly. "There is something on this desert besides us—something invisible."

"Ng . . ." Crustabread spoke into the awed silence. "Ng
. . . there is a commonsense explanation. Ng . . . the pit
was here when we came through the tunnel—dug by some
desert creature to reach the white root. We frightened it
away. When Scumble came down the slope the second time,
he simply mistook his direction and arrived at the pit, which
he hadn't seen before. The glimmer he saw was the sun
glancing on the desert creature's eyes, for of course it had
been waiting for the chance to come back for its food."

It was the longest speech any of them had ever heard

from Crustabread. His quiet voice carried so much authority that even Scumble was convinced, for the moment, that he had mistaken his direction down the slope.

They lugged the heavy root up to their camp. It had a shiny white rind and was almost round—"like the moon," Silky said. "It's a moon-melon. Do you think it's good to eat?"

Scumble shrugged. "Don't know. Can't tell yet." He pressed his knife down on the shiny rind, but the blade only bounced off, leaving not so much as a dent. He tried boring with the sharp point of the knife, and then he jabbed with it. There was no penetrating the stubborn covering.

"Wait a minute," said Crustabread. He pulled his sword out of its sheath and brought it down on the desert melon.

The two halves sprang apart with a shower of milky drops. An instant later the five New Heroes sprang apart, coughing and gasping and clutching their noses. A putrid smell of rotting vegetation rose from the moon-melon so thick that it was almost visible.

"Get rid of it!" Gam Lutie spluttered.

"It's *horrible!*" cried Silky, pressing her cloak over her nose.

But Scumble, deciding that the smell was no more penetrating than fish oil, though admittedly of a different variety, was already examining the fleshy meat of the melon. What would Muggles make of it, he wondered. *Unripe brings gripe.* Well, there was one thing you could say with assurance about this melon—it was not unripe.

But what about—*Bitter makes eyes glitter?* Gingerly he poked his forefinger at the pulp and then licked the juice from it. He had drawn his brows down in concentration, but now they shot up.

Confidently, he cut a chunk with his knife and raised it to his lips. Only then did he become aware of the horrified faces about him.

"You're not going to eat it!" Silky exclaimed.

"You're *not* going to eat it!" declared Gam Lutie.

"*I* wouldn't eat it," said Glocken.

Crustabread only watched him.

Scumble gave a little preparatory swallow. "We'll never know if someone doesn't taste it," he quavered. "Only think! If it *is* eatable, it means both food and drink!" He looked round at them, but their faces were no help, so before he could lose his nerve, he shut his eyes and plunged the morsel into his mouth. The juice trickled like honeyvine nectar down his throat, cooling, refreshing, soothing. Just at first he could taste the smell of it, so to speak, but after that— Recklessly, he cut another piece and popped it in after the first.

No one else would touch the melon, but Scumble ate a good quarter of it. You didn't notice the smell once you had actually eaten of the pulp. But though he urged the others to try, they only backed off, holding their noses. Scumble was used to that. Shrugging, he pressed the two half-rinds together and stored them in the tunnel.

Glocken and Crustabread had found a rusty stream of water trickling from the mountain, not tasty but all right for bathing. They went back to finish the ablutions Scumble had interrupted. Scumble offered to help Gam Lutie and Silky set out the food for their evening meal, but Silky said,

"Oh do go away, Scumble. You're taking my appetite. That melon is worse than fish oil."

Obediently, Scumble turned and walked with melancholy step down the slope. Would there ever be someone to get past the smell of him to the heart of him? He liked to think that if his heart had a smell, it would be of honeyvine. But folk didn't—

His next step encountered nothing but space. He tried to throw himself backwards, but his other foot skittered out from under him and he was suddenly sliding, sliding. He landed with an "Urrk!" of surprise at the bottom of the same mysteriously dug pit from which he had taken the melon.

Feeling foolish as well as a bit frightened, he hastily scrambled out of the hole. But the jolt had set his mind to thinking—about the moon-melon, the hole, the shimmer and stillness. With a brisk nod of his head, he padded over to the nearest melon plant and scraped at the soil around it with his fingers. He did the same thing to the plant beside it, and to another one beside that. Gradually, he worked his way back up the slope, stopping at every scraggly melon plant, no matter how small, to scrape at the soil. When he got back to the tunnel entrance, he found Gam Lutie watching him, her mouth tightened into a derisive smile. He pretended not to notice.

The evening meal was a silent affair. They partook of half the fish cakes which Muggles had packed, saving the rest for the morning. Scumble humbly offered the moon-melon, but no one was willing to taste it.

"No thank you," said Silky, delicately holding her nose, "and I really preferred you when you smelled of fish."

Gam Lutie ordered Scumble to get the melon out of nose-length, for she said the whole tunnel smelled of rotting vegetation. So Scumble obediently sat a little apart from the others and savored the melon to himself while the rest gazed out upon the sinking sun and looked mournful.

When night came, it dropped like a pulled window-shade. The sun slid out of sight as though jerked by a string, and there was a shiver in the air. Nobody argued when Crustabread suggested that they sleep inside the tunnel with the boulder pulled across the entrance. After they had moved their packs and supplies back into the safety of the tunnel, they shoved and tugged and pulled the boulder into place. In complete darkness they wrapped themselves in their cloaks and sought sleep.

After a while the little growlings and grumblings and yawnings stopped, and Scumble felt himself drifting off. Later, he woke to the sound of shuffling, but it was Glocken, who couldn't sleep and was going farther into the tunnel with a lighted candle to write in the scroll that Walter the Earl had given him.

He woke up again when Glocken came back to bed. It had grown colder, and he scrunched himself smaller in his cloak. He had a dream of shadowy gray-brown figures digging into the iron ground. The scratching, scraping sound of the diggers was so realistic that he half woke up before sinking back into the same dream once more.

After that he slept soundly.

He woke up stiff and cramped and cold. Gam Lutie and Crustabread were already up, and Glocken was stirring. Silky had to be poked and pulled from sleep.

Light slitted through little chinks around their boulder-door, just enough so that they could unscramble themselves without stepping on each other or on the heap they had made of their packs and swords the night before.

"Ready to roll back the door?" Crustabread's voice boomed against the walls.

They lined up in front of the boulder, their sore muscles tensed for the strain of heaving.

"One, two, three—heave!" They flung themselves against the rock.

With a terrible shock the boulder flew out and away from them, and they were catapulted into space like a handful of pebbles.

6

To dig a pit
Takes quite a bit
Of Digger hum and gristle.

To fill the hole
Takes greater toll
Of Glocken's peal and whistle.

—Gummy, *Scribbles*, Scroll Two
(Collected Works)

Silky felt nothing but a mild surprise as she went hurtling through the air. Birds do this, she told herself musingly.

The next moment, unlike the birds, she landed on the hard-baked ground with a bone-rattling jar. Her head went scrambly for a moment, and she dared not open her eyes. *I'm going to hurt dreadfully*, she thought. *Much more than from walking all day yesterday. I won't move because it will hurt so much.* . . .

Gradually she became aware of a whimpering that was going on almost in her ear, a piteous crying that wrung her heart. The air above and around her echoed the crying. It was like—it was like the sad softness of autumn rain on fallen leaves.

With a tremendous effort she unclosed her eyes the merest slit, but what she saw through the spinning couldn't be true, and she clamped her eyes shut again. What she *thought*

73

she saw was a sheer towering wall, as though she was in a deep pit dug out of the earth.

Meanwhile, the whimpering grew louder and louder. With a strength she didn't know she had, Silky sat bolt upright, clutching at her head to still its spinning. She *was* in a pit, a tremendous pit. High above was the mouth of the tunnel—she could actually see Gam Lutie's treasure hamper teetering on the brim—and around her were strewn the limp bodies of the others.

"Glocken!" she croaked, horrified. "Crustabread. . . ." Were they all dead? "Gam Lutie . . . Scumble. . . ."

The dreadful whimpering was going on and on in her ear. She twisted her head painfully to see where it was coming from.

The boulder—the door they had pushed away from the tunnel entrance—was lying beside her. And pinned under it . . .

He was small and the color of dust, his spidery-thin arms and body covered with a soft fuzz. Out of his wizened little face with its almost-nose, his greeny eyes melted with pain.

"Oh!" Silky gasped, and struggled to her feet. "Glocken! Crustabread! Come help!"

But help had already arrived. With gentle plopping sounds, four creatures like the first, but bigger, almost as tall as Silky herself, dropped into the pit. There were more ploppings as new arrivals plummeted down. They stood or crouched where they landed, keening over the baby under the rock.

"Well, do something!" Silky cried, forgetting to be afraid in the face of those piteous greeny eyes of the creature fastened under the rock. "If it's you who've been doing all the digging, you can dig him out!"

But the creatures stood helplessly round the rock, and their keening rose louder into the air.

"Stop that!" Silky ordered. "Stop it at once and *dig!*" She might as well have been talking to the dusty gray plants of the waste. With a groan of frustration she pushed futilely against the heavy boulder.

Instantly, the gray-brown creatures sprang to her side and began to push at the rock. In a trice they had rolled it away from the injured one, and Silky knelt by his side. But before she could more than glance at the poor mashed leg, she had to spring up once more and race after the other creatures. They were rolling the boulder round and round the pit, their faces happy and the keening turned into a humming.

"Stop! Stop!" Silky shrieked. "You'll crush somebody."

They rolled on, humming joyfully. They missed Scumble's head by a hair, but Gam Lutie lay directly in their path.

Silky reached them a fraction of a second before Gam Lutie could be rolled flat as a pat-cake. In desperation she did the only thing she could think of that might show the wild creatures what she wanted them to do. She drummed on the top of the boulder with the flat of her hands.

They forgot the game of push-the-boulder and began to drum. They drummed, and they hummed, and their wizened faces were blissful.

"Too much noise," groaned Gam Lutie through the drumming.

"What's happened?" demanded Scumble weakly. He had pushed himself up on one elbow.

75

"Everything," said Silky. "See to Glocken and Crusta-bread." She hurried back to the injured creature. His eyes were closed, and his little face had a greenish tinge. Biting her lower lip to keep from going giddy, Silky began to clean the wounded leg as best she could with the end of her sash. When the little creature moaned, she glanced swiftly at the other gray-brown figures around the boulder. Several of them had stopped drumming and were watching her anxiously.

"Scumble," Silky called softly, "go show them how to drum again, and be quick!"

In a moment the sound was deafening. It was all around and above them. Rimming the pit were dozens, perhaps even hundreds, more of the gray-brown creatures, and they were thrumming and humming in time with their fellows below. Bits of earth began to filter into the pit as they pounded on the ground.

"I hope they stay friendly. What are they?" It was Glocken, swaying toward her on unsteady legs.

Silky lifted her shoulders. "Diggers. Or Hummers. Or Drummers. But this little one is hurt—we've got to do something for him."

Glocken looked at the other Diggers, or Hummers, or Drummers. "*They* don't seem to be worrying overmuch."

"Oh, but they are. You should have heard them crying when they saw him under the rock. It's just that they're not very strong on wits, and they get distracted easily. Glocken, I need some clean cloth to bind up this leg."

He stared at her. "What do you expect me to do—give you my shirt?"

"A hand's width across the bottom will do. You'll never miss it."

It grew hotter by the moment in the pit, though the sun was still the other side of the mountain and they were in shadow. They had had no breakfast, nor even a drop of water, and the fine dust raised by the many feet trampling in the pit got into their eyes and noses and mouths.

Crustabread was pacing worriedly round the walls of their prison. Several of the Diggers left off their drumming and fell in behind him, then more and more until there was a solemn procession circling the pit.

Gam Lutie's voice rose in a quaver. "We'll cook to death when the sun gets above. What I can't understand—" Her eyes fell on Scumble, and understanding flashed into them. "You, Scumble, you did this to us! You were scratching around those horrid melon plants last night so that these beasts would dig them out for you! And now look at our plight!"

"I'm looking," said Scumble morosely. "Though I wouldn't call them beasts. That one tagging behind Crustabread looks remarkably like the mayor of Slipper-on-the-Water. He only wants a beard and a proper cloak. . . . Wait!" Ignoring Gam Lutie's gasp, Scumble sprang at the wall behind her. "Somebody help!" he panted. "Here's breakfast!" He was tugging at a knobby something that protruded from the side of the pit.

A dozen gray-brown spidery arms attacked the wall. Within moments their fingerpoints had torn out the moonmelon, and it went rolling and bouncing across the pit.

There was no question this time about eating the melon.

Indeed, Glocken gave a weak cheer, but was silenced in mid-voice by Crustabread's dry, "I don't suppose any of the swords fell down with us?"

They looked at each other blankly. The swords were all neatly piled in the tunnel three body-lengths above.

Scumble picked up the heavy moon-melon and staggered over with it to the mayor-like creature. "Master Mayor," he said ingratiatingly, "would you mind taking the rind off this fruit you dug for us?" Balancing it in one hand, he scraped at it with the other.

The Digger immediately sent his probing fingers into the melon and ripped off the rind.

"That's enough," Scumble said with alarm as the fingers advanced again. "Here, do some more wall, that's a good body." And he hastily made digging motions at the wall with his free hand. Master Mayor enthusiastically attacked the wall, and the rest joined in. Those who couldn't get digging space in the crush clambered up over the heads of the others, carrying loose clods out of the pit.

The New Heroes scarcely noticed the disagreeable smell of the moon-melon. To their parched throats it was balm, and they sucked greedily at the pulp. Silky managed to get some of the juice down the throat of the injured baby Digger. "He *is* a baby," she said. "See how small he is. And his fingerpoints are soft, not hard like the others." She winced as the soft fingerpoints accidentally scraped her arm, and quickly hid the red weal under her cloak.

"I wonder," said Crustabread quietly, "how we are going to get out?"

The slurruping noises gave over to startled silence. Eyes lifted and mouths dropped open.

"Why. . . ."'Glocken's voice deserted him before it had half-begun.

Gam Lutie was staring at the Diggers, who were bliss-fully carving out the wall as high as they could reach. They sounded like a swarm of bees in a hollow tree on a flower-filled afternoon.

"If we just let the Digger-things go on digging in that spot," she said, "the top part will cave in after a while, and we can walk out."

"But they would be buried alive!" cried Silky.

"Those Diggers up on top"—said Scumble slowly—"if we could get them to fill in this pit. . . ."

Gam Lutie gave him a squashing look. "*We* would be buried alive."

Scumble smiled apologetically. "I was only thinking that we would have to hoist somebody to the top to direct the operation. . . ."

They stared at him without comprehension until suddenly Glocken gave a gleeful yell. "That's it!" He clapped Scumble on the back so hard that the fish-presser toppled over.

It was a little while before they could carry out the plan, for Master Mayor, distracted by Glocken's action, forgot his wall-digging and struck his neighbor on the back. In a moment the Diggers were a whirlwind of flying hands and sprawling bodies.

"Stop them!" cried Silky. "They'll hurt each other!"

With a bound, Glocken was at the side of the nearest Digger. He seized the upraised arm firmly and began to hop up and down. The Digger fell into step immediately, and seconds later the battlefield had turned into a dancing exercise, with its own music.

Amidst the happy buzz of the occupied Diggers, the Minnipins went to work. Crustabread and Scumble planted themselves beneath a likely-looking section of the wall, and Glocken clambered up on their shoulders. He teetered there until his outstretched hands grasped two projections above his head, and his toes found niches that would hold them. Like a huge night-mouse spread on the wall, he clung there while Crustabread and Scumble hoisted Silky and Gam Lutie to their shoulders.

"Hurry," Glocken urged. "My eyeballs are p-popping."

When the pyramid was finally in position, Glocken transferred first one foot from its niche to Silky's swaying shoulder and then the other to Gam Lutie's. Cautiously he straightened, pulling himself upright with his hands. Dirt crumbled under his fingers and showered into the eyes and mouths of those below.

There was a pause when Glocken got as high as he could reach, and then he said, "Brace your heads against the wall."

Before anybody could protest, he stepped squarely on top of Silky's head. She thought her neck must surely break under the strain, but she dug her fingers into the wall until they went numb. Dimly through her welling tears she could see the Diggers scrambling easily over each other up the side of the pit. The hums swelled as they found delight in this latest game, and though the base of their pyramid kept walking away from the job, it made no difference. The Diggers clambered up and down the walls as easily as they moved on level ground.

Then Glocken got his other foot on Gam Lutie's head. The whole pyramid shook and swayed again, and for a moment Glocken half-crouched, clutching at the wall. He groped upward with his free arm and at last fastened upon another moon-melon.

He was not a moment too soon. The human ladder shuddered violently and came apart all at once. Bodies went tumbling and rolling to the ground. But Glocken was high on the wall and clinging to the moon-melon. As the others were still painfully picking themselves up, he drew himself half a length higher. A minute later he was over the edge and out. The Diggers forsook their own pyramid game and easily scaled the wall after him.

A moment later the dirt began to fly. At first the Diggers simply shoveled in all directions, but after a while Glocken got them better organized. They pushed the chunks and clods into the pit from one side for a while and then moved round to the other side to raise the level there. Below, the Minnipins with the baby Digger switched from level to higher level. Clouds of dust choked the air, but the Diggers hummed with the joy of working, and Glocken marked time with a chant:

"Silver bells,
Golden bells,
Shining bells,
Olden bells. . . ."

The sun was high in the white-hot sky when a break came in the rhythm. Without warning to the Minnipins in the pit, the rain of dirt changed into a hail of husked moon-melons hurtling from every direction, the air rotten-sweet with their smell as they burst and splattered. Scumble finally managed to catch one that sent him sprawling on his back.

For a delicious space of time there was nothing to be heard but sucking sounds above and below, as Diggers and Minnipins refreshed themselves. Then—

"Here they come again!" announced Scumble needlessly, as a clod sailed past his ear.

A weary hour later, four Minnipins straggled out of the pit on the downside. It would be some time still before the hole would be filled in enough for them to get to the tunnel, but here they could breathe a little easier, and they weren't in danger of being bashed by a flying clod. There were easily two hundred of the Diggers crammed together round the pit, bent over with their backs to the hole and paddling the dirt between their legs, their scrawny arms going so fast that they were blurs. Glocken paced behind them, his face dirt-stained and as red as boiled blood-root. There was a wicked scratch down one cheek, as though he had got in the way of a fingerpoint. His voice was hoarse, but still he chanted:

> "Whispering bells,
> Kispering swells,
> Who knows where
> The first Glocken dwells?"

Another hour steamed away. Silky comforted the whimpering baby Digger as best she could. She felt dried out and shrunken, like a strip of salt trout preserved over the winter. Even her eyeballs gritted under her eyelids. It was no wonder the Diggers were so spidery. If Minnipins were to live in this parched land, would they too dry up to old soft leather? Or would they merely die?

Silky shivered in the heat. Even if they survived this terrible day, how could they hope to make the two-day journey through this sunstruck land to the mouth of the Watercress!

A sudden hoarse shout roused her from her gloomy forebodings.

"Stop! and *rest*," Glocken was crying. "Stop! and *rest*."

The way was filled in! It was done! Glocken had done it. The way was filled in, and they could go back to the tunnel —if Glocken could stop the diggers before they filled *that* in. And then—surely then, they would keep on going until they came out of the old gold mine back into the Land Between the Mountains. . . .

"Stop! and *rest*." Now Glocken was flinging his hands up at "Stop!" and stamping his feet in time to "and *rest*."

Master Mayor looked up from his dirt-throwing, cocked his head to one side. An instant later he was flinging his hands up and stamping his feet in the easy rhythm that Glocken had started.

"Stop! and *rest.*"

One by one and then five by ten, the Diggers left their pit-filling and joined in the new dance. Their humming filled the desert with happy sound. When the last Digger had thrown the last clod of earth and taken up the new game, Glocken made them an elaborate bow and said, "Thank you, good friends. Let's *all* rest."

His eyes rolled up in his head, and he pitched forward to the ground.

When the night falls down
And the stars shine bright,
The desert grows stark
In the stone-cold light.

When the day dawns gold
And the sun strikes straight,
The desert then shimmers
Like a white-hot grate.

When Minnipins travel
In the desert far away,
They shiver in the night
And simmer in the day.

> —Gummy, *Scribbles*, Scroll Two
> (Collected Works)

With a cry Silky struggled to her feet, but Crustabread put a hand on her arm.

"Wait."

Master Mayor wavered uncertainly for a moment, and then he too executed a sort of bow and stretched his length on the ground. Like a field of dusty grain blown before the wind, the other Diggers went flat. In a moment there was nothing to be seen save the Watercress green that was Glocken's cloak, for the bodies of the Diggers blended uncannily with the gray-brown land.

It's no wonder, Silky thought, *it's no wonder we didn't see them at the beginning. They must have been all around when we came out of the tunnel. And if it hadn't been for the little one caught fast under the rock.* . . . . She clasped the tiny creature closer. If it hadn't been for the baby keeping them on the spot, the Diggers might just have gone away, leaving five Minnipins to perish at the bottom of the pit.

"All right." Crustabread let out his breath in a long sigh. "Step carefully. Go directly to the tunnel. I'll fetch Glocken with Scumble."

"Surely she's not taking that creature along!" Gam Lutie's voice was starched with unbelief.

Without a word Silky elbowed past her with the baby Digger and stumbled along the slope to the tunnel's entrance.

The air of the tunnel blew cool and dank against their sun-blistered faces and enveloped them like softest sarcen garments. Silky sank down gratefully against the cold wall and let the air wash over her. If only she never had to move again! The baby Digger in her arms stirred and began to whimper.

"Oh *can't* you stop that!" she cried in despair. For just an instant she wished she had listened to Gam Lutie and left the creature outside. But it was only an instant. She held him closer to make up for the hard thought.

"Poor little wafer," she murmured. "Why, that's what I'll call you—Wafer!" She took a deep breath of the delicious cool air to brace herself. "And now we're going to do something about that leg!"

"I trust that by 'we' you don't mean *me*," said Gam Lutie

sourly. "You'll soon get tired of playing nurse. I can tell you now. A flitter-wing like you."

Silky scorned to answer. Her eyes had grown used to the dimness of the tunnel, so that she could make out the outlines of the herb basket sitting alongside the packs. Holding tightly to the frail Wafer, she crawled over to it and, grasping the handle, dragged it to the mouth of the tunnel, where the sunlight streamed along the floor.

One by one she took up the pots and jars and packets to read the labels written in Muggles' untidy hand. What would Muggles choose from all these unguents and potions to put on the Wafer's leg? Silky glanced down at it and shivered with distaste. It was badly swollen now, and angry purplish streaks were shooting upward from the bandage. She turned back to the herbs. Here was willow essence and blood-root, tannybark and sassafras. And . . .

Her hand lingered on the tiny pot of white salve. It was all that remained of the precious store which Mingy had taken from the Mushrooms.

She began working the stopper out of the pot.

"You're not going to use *that!*" Gam Lutie declared.

Silky nodded.

"I cannot allow it. That salve might mean life or death to one of us. We're more important than a beast!"

"Not to the beast, we're not," said Silky. She suddenly realized that she was defying Gam Lutie. *Gam Lutie!* "There is enough for all if we use it sparingly," she added as a sort of apology. The stopper popped out.

"I can't permit it!" Gam Lutie's voice shrilled out of control. At the same moment her hand darted out to snatch at the tiny pot.

"Look out!" But Silky's warning came too late.

The pot flew out of her hand and shattered against the stone wall. The sound echoed back through the tunnel and went on for a long time, as though the pot was broken over and over again.

Silky lifted her eyes accusingly to Gam Lutie's furious face, and they stood there like that for long moments, while the Wafer cowered close to Silky.

Crustabread's voice broke the charged silence. "Make way! Make way!" A hulking shadow loomed at the mouth of the tunnel, and then Crustabread staggered inside with Glocken over his shoulder. Scumble stalked behind, his arms laden with shiny white moon-melons.

Gam Lutie sprang to help ease Glocken to the floor.

"He'll be all right," said Crustabread. "Too much sun and exertion. Best put some of that Mushroom salve on his scratches. Whoo!" He blinked round at them in the gloom. "What's wrong?"

Silky, who had knelt beside Glocken with the Wafer still clutched in her arms, said with no feeling in her voice, "Gam Lutie didn't want me to put the salve on the Wafer's leg and tried to take it from me. The pot broke."

"And I was right!" declared Gam Lutie. "We must be practical if we are to survive. The salve is for our use. Muggles gave it to *us*."

"Uh . . ." Scumble started, and fell silent. But nobody else said anything, so he tried again. "That is . . . although. . . ." Desperately, he scratched his head for inspiration. "I just happened to think of something Muggles said. About . . . about . . . well, she said, 'Both the fish and the fisherman think the river is theirs.' That's what she said," he added lamely.

"I fail to see what fish has to do with Mushroom salve." Gam Lutie gave him a look of disgust.

"Well, uh. . . . I wondered if just perhaps the salve belongs to anybody, who, uh, needs it. . . ."

"Like me," came a feeble voice. "Why doesn't somebody scrape up the salve that's left and put it on my scratches!"

"I'll do it," said Silky. She made a little nest of her cloak for the Wafer and then set to work scraping up what she could from the scattered shards of the pot. What a great thing it would be if they could find the plant it came from! There would never be any quarrels then about who could use it. It was easy to be generous when you had a lot of anything. The pinch came when you had to divide not-enough.

Silky sat back on her heels and rubbed her forehead with the back of her hand. She wasn't used to thinking, and it made her feel rather tired.

Glocken gave a large groan. Hastily Silky began painting the scratches on his face with the scraped-up salve. When she had them well-covered, there was still a little ointment left.

She hesitated, then resolutely knelt beside the tiny Digger and with gentle fingers removed the bandage. The greeny eyes were clouded with pain, but there was trusting watchfulness in their depths.

"Poor Wafer," she murmured. "I'll make you better. I promise you." But she didn't like the look of the useless leg. If only one of them knew more about such things! If only

Gam Lutie hadn't made her drop the Mushroom salve! If only Muggles were here! If only. . . . With a start, she pulled the herb kit closer to rummage in it. Thinking of Muggles had reminded her of the Book of Muggles' Maxims. Perhaps it really would give her some good advice. Fetching it out of the herb basket, she balanced it on her hands and let it open at random. Her eyes fell on:

No use casting after a fish that is already halfway down-stream. Bend your mind to catching the next one.

That wasn't much help! She wasn't thinking of going fishing. She only wanted to know what to do about the Wafer's leg. Frowning, she opened the *Maxims* to another page. *Crying over a skimpy meal only oversalts the little that is there.*

Really! What did oversalting have to do with an injured leg! She would give the book one more try. Setting it on its spine, she let it spring open where it would. This time she got: *If wishes were cobblestones, there would be no grass.*

Annoyed, she chunked the *Maxims* back into the herb basket. Cobblestones! Crying over meals! Casting after fish! She was only wasting her time. Instead of maundering on about "what if this" and "what if that" and looking in books for advice, she should just do the best she could with what she had! That decided, she spread the remainder of the salve on the injured leg and made the cloak-nest more comfortable for the Wafer. Then she stirred round in the herb basket, looking for she knew not what.

Her hand fell upon a stone bottle labeled "Essence of Sleep." As good as any, she thought. Reaching for her water bottle, she poured a dollop into the clay medicine cup, measured into it three drops of the essence, and stirred. When she offered the mixture to the Wafer, he made a face like any Minnipin child and tried to spew it out, but she urged it on him until he at last swallowed some.

Crustabread and Scumble ventured forth to fetch a bottle of the brackish water for herb tea while Gam Lutie made a cooking fire of one of the round bushes. Nobody had much appetite for the fare in their packs, and they ate mechanically, saying little. There was some discussion about eating the fishcakes. "Muggles said they would spoil," insisted Scumble. "We were supposed to eat the last of them this morning."

But after sniffing at them and taking experimental nibbles, they decided that the fishcakes had not yet spoiled, and they consumed as many as they were able, with no ill effects.

"It is my opinion," observed Gam Lutie, "that the one called Muggles is full of meaningless advices."

And Silky, though she wasn't inclined to echo Gam Lutie just then, had to agree.

They kept a watchful eye on the Diggers outside, or at least on the spot where they had left the Diggers fast asleep, for there was no distinguishing them from the gray-brown ground. As Glocken pointed out, they ought to sleep a good long time, for they had spent last night digging the pit and most of the day filling it in.

"As for me," he said, stretching lazily, "I feel more than somewhat recovered. After a good sleep, I'll be able to go on." He rolled over, pulling his cloak round him.

"We'll call you at sundown," announced Crustabread.

"No need." Glocken gave a shuddering yawn. "A sunset

is a pretty thing, but I don't mind missing—*What do you mean, sundown?*"

"That's when we march," said Crustabread.

The western sky was still tinged with pink when they stole from the dark security of the tunnel to strike south along the base of the mountain.

Their departure was not without argument.

"Ng. . . ." Crustabread gulped as he saw Gam Lutie setting out the hamper containing the bronze chest. "Ng . . . perhaps the time has come to stow the treasure in the tunnel. We must travel light."

Gam Lutie gave him a shriveling look. "It is *quite* out of the question."

"Ng . . ." He tried once more. "You may be endangering all our lives."

"Not I," said Gam Lutie. She pointed an accusing finger at Silky, who was preparing to gather up the little Wafer, now heavily asleep. "There's the one. Silky *must* leave that creature behind."

"No!" cried Silky.

"Don't be foolish!" said Glocken. "We don't know how the Diggers will feel about our carrying one of them off with us."

"Better let each kind take care of its own," Crustabread said. "We'll put him with the rest of the Diggers where they will find him."

"But he can't keep up with them!" protested Silky. "They will go off carelessly without him, and he'll die all alone."

"Be practical," said Gam Lutie. "He would have died by now, anyway, if you hadn't put our salve on him."

Scumble cleared his throat. "I agree. Put the creature beside his kind. Now then. Let's get started. Where's that hamper?"

Silky looked from one to the other. Every heart was turned against her and the little creature. Heart! They had *stones* in their breasts!

She gave the sleeping Wafer a last lingering stroke before placing him near the other Diggers and then padded silently after Crustabread, Glocken, and Gam Lutie, their figures already dim in the fast-approaching darkness. Scumble brought up the rear, but she didn't wait for him. Miserable, toadying fish-presser. He would rather curry favor with Gam Lutie than save the Wafer's life.

Stars glittered like frost crystals above them, so close at hand in the clear air that they wanted to be plucked. After a long time the moon rose, and though they still tramped along in the sharp shadow cast by the mountains to their left, the moon-frozen waste stretched out eerily beside them, flat, barren and hostile. Not a thorn stirred. Not a sound disturbed the empty air beyond the pad of their own feet and their heavy breathing.

The night grew colder and still colder. With numb fingers Silky pulled her cloak closer round her and struggled on, her feet leaden, her toes without feeling. Her mouth was parched, and she thought longingly of the cool fibrous moon-melon, lost to them now because they had left the Diggers behind. No one had thought to pack the melons Scumble had brought into the tunnel. Not even Scumble himself, that miserable pack-toad.

When the moon finally topped the mountains, Crusta-bread called a short halt.

"We'll eat a crust and have a sip of water from our bottles. But only a sip," he cautioned them. "There has been no water since the small stream near the tunnel, and we can't be sure of finding more until we reach the mouth of the Watercress. That means we cannot eat salted fish unless we find water to quench our thirst. Is that clear?"

With fingers like sticks Silky undid her pack and found the bottle of sweet Watercress water Muggles had put there. How much was a sip when your throat was dried to powder? Surely more than when you were sitting quietly at home by the fire having a cup of hot tea. She let the water slosh into her mouth, but not until she had stoppered the bottle once more did she allow it to trickle on down her throat. It was like putting a drop of water on a hot fire.

"That's enough, Glocken," came Crustabread's stern voice.

"You're wrong," said Glocken with a croak. "It's not nearly enough." But he took the bottle from his mouth and stoppered it. "Heigh! Look at Scumble! Wake up, Scumble, and have your drink."

But Scumble didn't stir. He was sprawled on the ground like a pile of laundry.

Alarm beat its wings in Silky's throat. What was wrong with him? Why didn't somebody look after him? Angrily, because nobody made a move, she took herself stumblingly over to his side and shook him. When he still didn't stir, she pulled his head up. He only groaned. Then she noticed how he had clasped his hands to his body. But what she saw when she turned them over made her angrier than ever. The

palms were raw where the basket handle had rubbed them, and his fingers were stiffened into claws.

"It's your own foolish fault," she railed at him. "If Gam Lutie can't sleep soundly without her treasure, let her carry it herself!"

Scumble only looked dumbly at her.

She treated his hands with good herb ointment, which she found in the herb basket, and bound them round and round with the roll of reed gauze. By this time the others had come to life enough to help. Glocken gave Scumble a swallow of water, and Gam Lutie silently passed over a hunk of bread.

Minutes before, Silky had been ready to drop like a stone, but now fury held her up. Fury at all of them for being so—so *lumpish*. At least *one* of the party should be looking ahead, planning, finding water or food or the plant that the Mushroom salve came from. Very well, if nobody else would do anything, then she, Silky, must.

She marked one of the great prickly bushes for attack and brought her sword slicing down on it, marveling at the suppressed power of the blackened blade. The severed wands oozed liquid, and a pungent, slightly bitter scent wafted her way.

"Don't touch it!"

Silky dropped the sword in fright.

"Don't touch it!" Crustabread came running like a twitch-whisker over to her. "Can't you *smell* it?" He jerked her away from the plant.

Silky pulled her arm from his grasp. "Really, Crustabread. It doesn't smell any worse than fish oil or moon-melon. In fact, a whole lot better."

"It's a death-plant!" Crustabread's usually quiet woods-voice was hoarse with feeling. "Believe me, and never touch anything that smells like that."

Silky felt a moth of fear trace over the back of her neck, but she said defiantly, "There's no need to yank and shove, is there? Sometimes you act demented, Crustabread." She picked up the sword and stamped back to get her pack to-gether. In a moment the others stopped staring at her and got their packs ready too.

When they left the spot, Silky gave the death-plant a

wide berth. The smell of it she would not now forget—a sharp and acrid odor that spoke of death. The sudden shiver that traveled her spine had nothing to do with the cold night.

The ragged file trailed on and on through the icy moonlight, Crustabread still at the head, Scumble still bringing up the rear and still obstinately carrying Gam Lutie's basket in spite of Glocken's offer to take it. The landscape was everlastingly the same: the toppling reaches of mountain on the left, the unceasing plain on the right. The silence was so profound that after a while it seemed like a sound in itself. You could imagine that you were hearing all sorts of things in a silence like this. Once Silky stopped short, and Scumble almost fell over her.

"I—I thought I heard a cry," she whispered.

Scumble merely grunted, and they plodded on in the deafening moon-bound silence.

They scanned the side of the mountain anxiously for a cave that would shelter them from the coming day's sun, but there was nothing save unending sheer walls. There was not so much as an overhanging rock. The vast white melon of a moon inched down the sky, and still they picked up their feet and put them down, like stick dolls being walked by children.

It was not till the melon was riding low in the west that Crustabread called another halt. Silently they huddled together for warmth and chewed with parched mouths on dry bread.

"How far are we from the tunnel?" Scumble asked suddenly.

"Too far to turn back," said Crustabread. His eyes were

brooding. "Unless we find a cave to shelter in, we'll have to keep marching until the heat of the sun stops us."

Glocken gave a groan from the soles of his feet.

"And what then?" demanded Gam Lutie.

"Then . . ." said Crustabread slowly, ". . . then we hope that we can endure until the sun sets again. And again . . . and again. . . . We know not how many nights' walkings we are from the end of our journey. Look." He pulled the spade-pick from Scumble's pack, and with the sharp point he scraped a rough map on the ground. It was like the map Walter the Earl had chalkstoned on Muggles' hearth.

Crustabread tapped his stick on the circle. "Here is Slipper-on-the-Water, and here"—drawing the stick along to the cross at the top—"here is our first day's journey that brought us through the tunnel in the mountains. This cross down here marks our present location, as nearly as I can reckon."

"But then," said Silky, "it can't be more than another night's journey to the mouth of the Watercress!"

"Of course!" said Gam Lutie. "You can *see* how close we are!"

Crustabread slowly shook his head. "Ng . . . the mountains on my map are only the way we *hoped* they would be. A neat little circle round our valley with the wasteland stretching out in all directions. A simple journey of three days round the outside to the mouth of the Watercress." He drew a deep breath. "But look up there!" He swung the spade-pick to point at the mountains towering over them.

It took time for his words' meaning to soak into their frozen minds. The mountains . . . what had he said about the mountains . . . ? Silky caught her breath. The mountains were all wrong! That was it! The map showed them curving off toward the mouth of the Watercress River, but they didn't do that. They didn't do that at all. Silky bit her lip to keep from crying out.

For the mountains marched, an unbroken barrier, as far as the eye could see—straight on . . . and on . . . and on. . . .

8

Once upon a whisper-time—so it is said but who
would believe it?—long before the Minnipins
reached the Land between the Mountains, the
Glocken of Then played upon his bells and the
beetle-bores, which had come to infest the coun-
tryside, fell upon their backs and waggled their
legs for a space and died. But the smell of dead
beetle-bore was great, and the bells could do
nothing about that, and *this* I believe.

—Pretend-story told by Glocken
to Glocken to Glocken, from
Then to Now

Bleakly staring at the mountain barrier flung against the
sky, Gam Lutie felt a tremor of—could it be fear? Of course
not, she told herself, but the tremor persisted, quivering up
from her middle into her very throat. Fear? Gam Lutie
afraid? Unthinkable!

"I expect," someone was saying, "that is, I really do think
it is time to open this hamper."

Gam Lutie snapped her eyes away from the fearsome
Barrier. "Don't speak foolishness at such a time!"

But Scumble had already thrown back the cover of the
hamper.

"Have you left your senses behind?" demanded Gam Lutie. "Close up the treasure this—" The thin, whimpering cry from the hamper cut her off.

"Oh Scumble!" Silky cried. "Oh Scumble! You brought him!" Falling to her knees before the hamper, she tenderly lifted out the baby Digger. He blinked round at them with frightened greeny eyes.

Gam Lutie's throat went dry. The treasure . . . the treasure that was forever to be in her keeping, that she had brought so carefully with her to preserve it from harm. . . .

"Oh Scumble," Silky stopped her crooning sounds over the spidery creature long enough to say, "I can't tell you . . ."

"*I can.*" Gam Lutie had found her voice, and a terrible voice it was. "*Where is the treasure?*"

Scumble had the grace to look shamefaced. "Tunnel," he mumbled.

She wanted to beat her fists on his head . . . to grind him into the iron hard ground . . . to. . . . With a tremendous gasp, she got hold of herself. It took every fiber of will she possessed to control the furious pounding in her temples. When at last she could trust herself to speak again, she had to push the words out between her teeth.

"There . . . is . . . no trust . . . in you."

Crustabread looked from the hamper to her. "You are wrong," he said. "Scumble is all trust. None of the rest of us was thinking with his brain. We might have starved here."

"When you're hungry," said Scumble modestly, "it's better to think with your stomach." With a tug, he brought out of the hamper a large moon-melon and laid it carefully on

101

the ground. "There wasn't room for more than two." He had been avoiding Gam Lutie's eyes, but now he straightened and dared look back at her. "I'm sorry, Gam Lutie," he said after a nervous swallow. "I hid the bronze chest in a niche high up in the wall of the tunnel. I promise you it's safe."

"Shall I carve?" asked Glocken.

I won't eat of it, I won't, Gam Lutie repeated over and over to herself. *I will not be a partner to perfidy.* But when the pieces of melon were laid out, and the others respectfully waited for her to serve herself, her hand scarcely hesitated in reaching for a slice. Retiring a little from the rest, she forced herself to eat as though her throat wasn't a parched desert. Her aloofness had little effect on the others, who unashamedly slurped and gulped and smacked like noisy greedy sucking-fish.

Listen to their noise. . . . Listen. . . . Gam Lutie shrank back as she realized that her own lips were smacking over the melon as loudly as theirs. She must get hold of herself! She must!

They brought her fishcake and bread from their own shares, but she refused with what seemed the rightful degree of haughtiness, and then wished she had taken some, for her act of self-denial went unnoticed.

The moon was slipping away now, the earth darkening, and the cold more bitter. Only Gam Lutie's pride kept her from joining the huddled warmth of the others. Silky had wrapped the shivering baby Digger in a fold of her cloak, and she made odious cooing sounds over him the while she pushed bits of the moon-melon into his mouth. Glocken was fumbling with the scroll which Walter the Earl had given him, trying to make his numb fingers manage the charcoal-stick. Gam Lutie's eyes passed over Scumble the faithless.

Crustabread came to his feet, even in his weariness moving more like a woods animal than a Minnipin. "We must go on."

There was no argument. One by one they groaned upward, adjusted their packs. Silky laid the baby Digger in the hamper with the second moon-melon and lowered the lid. Without a word, Glocken picked up the hamper and plodded off after Crustabread. Gam Lutie fell in behind, then Silky, and last of all, Scumble.

They had picked their frozen way for perhaps half an hour when Glocken suddenly gave a great groan and doubled over, clutching his middle.

"What is it?" Gam Lutie hurried forward. "What's the matter with you?" She knelt beside him where he was squirming on the hard ground. Crustabread came running back.

"Something . . . biting . . . my middle," Glocken gasped. "Gam Lutie . . . I'm dying. . . ."

"Nonsense," said Gam Lutie with a certainty she wasn't at all certain of. She pushed his hair back and felt his forehead. Clammy. His feet suddenly thrashed out, and his whole middle arched like a bridge.

"What's wrong with him?" Silky whispered, horrified.

Gam Lutie pushed her aside. "I must have hot water, and at once. Crustabread, set fire to one of those dry, bushy plants. Silky, give me the herb basket. And get Glocken's water bottle out of his pack and wrap his cloak around him. Better get all the water bottles together and heat them—just in case."

"Just in case of *what?*" Silky's eyes were wide as she untied the herb basket from her belt.

"In case we need them. What else? Now move!" Gam Lutie tore at the fastenings of the herb basket. Fish cakes. She was sure it was the fish cakes, too long in the broiling sun at the tunnel's mouth yesterday. Fish-poisoning. Essence of Emptie, she muttered as she rummaged through the clay pots and bottles. Essence of Emptie. Her numbed fingers stumbled about until she found the right one. DANGER, shouted the label in blood-berry ink. NEVER USE FULL STRENGTH. USE ONLY IF ALL ELSE FAILS.

Idiot, Gam Lutie said between her teeth, if I wait to see all else failing, it will be too late for the Essence. Willing her hands to remain steady, she measured half a spoonful of the mud-brown liquid into the clay medicine cup.

Behind her, one of the dry bushes flamed up, and she heard Crustabread call to Scumble to uproot more of the bushes to feed the fire. The clinking sounds told her that Silky was propping the stone bottles around the flames.

Near at hand the baby Digger, spilled from the hamper when Glocken went sprawling, kept up a steady whimpering that grated on Gam Lutie's raw nerves.

Glocken suddenly began to shiver, but when Gam Lutie tried to wrap him closer in his cloak, he kicked it off again with his thrashing feet. When she tried to rub his icy hands, he jerked them away. Then Silky silently appeared and handed over a steaming flask wrapped round with folds of cloth. Carefully, Gam Lutie measured the water into the Essence of Emptie and watched it turn murky. She handed the flask back to Silky and waved her away.

"Glocken!" she commanded with all the authority in her,

"stop this silly groaning and take your medicine. Sit up and drink this." She yanked him upright, and when he opened his mouth to protest, poured the murky liquid down his throat. He coughed and sputtered, but the Essence of Emptie stayed down, and Gam Lutie sat back on her heels. He would be sick, and when his stomach was empty, he would recover. Probably.

The baby Digger whimpered louder, and Gam Lutie, irritated, called to Silky to see to him since she had appointed herself his caretaker. There was no answer.

"Silky!" she repeated, fear sharpening her voice.

Nothing, except—was that a little cry above the snapping of the fire?

Alarmed, Gam Lutie sprang to her feet and stared round her in the half-light of the coming dawn. The fire still blazed, and wisps of steam curled up from the stone flasks encircling it. But the other Minnipins had disappeared as though wiped off the face of the desert.

"Crustabread! Silky! Scumble! Answer me!" Her voice disappeared after them into the frozen loneliness.

She stood stock-still for an instant, the fear gnawing at her, and then, when she felt certain that she could keep her legs from running wildly into the desert, she snatched up the herb basket and a water flask and began to circle the burning bush. The lightening sky revealed nothing but the ghostly shapes of desert plants.

But then Glocken called feebly, and she had to hurry back to where he was staggering to his feet. She led him off a few steps and held his head while he was sick.

"Better," he gasped, leaning heavily against her. "Cold . . ." and he began to shiver violently.

She dragged him back to the fire and wrapped his cloak securely about him. He gave her a twist of a smile and closed his eyes.

This time she made a wider cast around the fire, and then a still wider one, fanning out farther and farther into the desert from the mountain's base. It wasn't until the next semicircle that she stumbled over Silky. She was doubled up on the ground on the far side of the fire, and her breathing came in stutters.

Gam Lutie went swiftly to work, her mind in a ferment of dread. If Silky was this bad, would Scumble and Crustabread still be alive when she found them? It was a punishment, of course. And a just one. They had left behind the treasure and punished themselves by eating bad fishcakes. Certainly it was only justice that they pay for their perfidy with sick stomachs. But death . . . ? She finally had to pry Silky's teeth apart with the spoon and pour the medicine mixture down her throat.

She spent another precious minute striking a spark to a nearby dry bush to mark the spot, and then she hurried on with her herb basket, in an ever-widening fan, to find Scumble and Crustabread. The desert was a lighter gray now. Time . . . time . . .

A moment later she came upon Scumble, but the sight of him was horrifying. He was draped headfirst over a plant— he must have toppled into it when the sickness had taken him. Dried blood caked a hundred punctures where the thorns had punctured his skin. Thorns . . . ! Gam Lutie choked back a cry, for Scumble had keeled over into a death-plant.

Setting her teeth, she went to work to disentangle him.

The thorns clung tenaciously to his clothing, resisting her pulls and tugs. She dared not think of what poisons were seeping into his blood. Her thoughts touched on the Mushroom salve that Silky had wasted on the baby Digger—and on the pot broken in the struggle for it—and shied away to Crustabread, still somewhere on the desert, still untreated. She raised her head to call out.

"Crustabread! Crustabread! Where are you!" But her voice was thin and useless in the vastness, and it ended on a sob.

Frenziedly she attacked the death-plant. Cruel barbs slashed at her, tore her hands. She ripped back, no longer caring what venoms she was releasing, only determined to overcome this baneful plant at last. But for every thorn that she pulled out of Scumble's clothes, two more snagged him. If she only had Hack the Butcher's long knife. . . .

Long knife. . . . Her jaw dropped. But she *had* a long knife—the sword of the Minnipins! What had gone wrong with her headpiece! She was acting as addled as a hooter-bird smoked out of a hollow tree.

The sword of the Minnipins sliced through the death-plant like a knife through a fresh stringy bean. In three whacks, Scumble came free from the plant's clutches and sagged against her. Dropping the sword, she lowered him to the hard ground and snatched the bottle of Essence from the herb basket.

He looked dead.

In desperation, Gam Lutie tilted the bottle and trickled Essence of Emptie directly into his mouth. NEVER USE FULL STRENGTH—the warning words shouted at her in the blood-berry ink. *I can't help it*, she half-sobbed, not knowing whether she spoke aloud or only thought the words. *He will surely die without it. If it burns out his voice, at least he will still live. . . .*

When she was sure that the Essence was down to stay, she tilted the water flask to Scumble's mouth to offset the searing effects of the strong medicine, but most of the water ran out. Gently she laid him on his side on the ground and struggled to her feet. There was nothing more she could do for him except to pluck the rest of the thorns from his clothing, and that could wait until she had found Crustabread. She knew it was surely too late to save Crustabread's life, but she must make the effort. She didn't take time to kindle another fire. There was enough light now to find her way back.

Grasping her sword and catching up the herb basket on the other arm, she struck out once more in an ever bigger arc from the mountain barrier.

They should never have come on this expedition, she thought bitterly. They weren't fitted for it. What could even a Gam Lutie do with a band of folk like these—fish oil, sarcen silk, and bells. And the other one? Who knew about Crustabread? He was silence and a queer little gulp. Despair seized her. Deep black despair such as she had never known, despair that was supposed to be alien to anybody carrying the Gam Lutie name. Was she no better then, under a desert sky, than a Scumble or a Glocken or even a flittery Silky? It was a galling thought.

After a while, between one dreary step and the next, she thought of the book of Muggles' *Maxims* in the herb basket. "When all is despair, open this book and read what is there." She had no faith in the simple Muggles' ability to overcome a Gam Lutie's despondency, but it cost little effort to extract the book from the basket and let it fall open in her hands. When this was done, she bent her head and read in the early light, *The turtle soup doesn't burn until all the liquor has boiled away.*

For a moment she didn't take it in and read it again, her cracked lips moving with the words. Then she gave a snort and clapped the book to. *Very* helpful! Turtle soup, really! Clearly, the Muggles one was not in possession of all her head elements.

In any case, now she knew where she stood—alone. It is where a Gam Lutie always stood. Alone and dependable. All was not lost so long as Gam Lutie was still able to move! She lifted her head and stepped out more determinedly. Her right hand had begun to tingle, and she switched the sword to her left.

A moment later she faltered to a halt and stood staring down at the sword. There could be no doubt. The tingling, now in her left hand, was coming from the sword's hilt. It was warm to the touch. And the blackened blade—wasn't it less black now? Fearfully, she raised her head and, turning in a slow circle, scanned the desert reaches. There was nothing—nothing except the Barrier on one side and the endless scrubby growth of the desert floor. Nothing moved—and yet the sword grew warm in her hand. It was the secret of the swords—the secret that told of danger nearby as clearly as a shout.

With a last anguished scanning of the ground round her for a sight of Crustabread, she turned and fled back to the thread of smoke that marked the first campfire. She must gather her patients together, try to rouse them. She. . . .

Suddenly her foot plunged through the hard crust of the earth, and she pitched to the ground, the sword knocked from her hand.

At the same moment an unearthly screech split the air.

Stumbling, scrambling, she wrenched her foot out of the hole . . . *hole!* . . . snatched up the sword, and stumbled on.

Another shrill scream. It was the baby Digger, struggling on the ground against a—a thing that tore at the dressings on his hurt leg.

Without any will on Gam Lutie's part, the sword lifted and fell, cleaving the thing in two.

She was too stunned for a moment to move. The two splits lay at her feet, but in her mind she could still see the thing whole—a crusty, greenish-brown egg shape, flatter on the bottom, about the size of one of Prize the Baker's loaves. Where the sword had cut it through, it leaked a thick white substance. Its tearing claws were folded now, but Gam Lutie remembered with a shudder how powerfully they had shredded the wrappings of the baby Digger's leg. It had a tail. . . . Fighting against the sick feeling inside her, Gam Lutie bent closer. The tail was in segments—like the vine of the wild grape—and it snaked across the ground as far as Gam Lutie could see.

She caught her breath. There beyond Glocken—a faint movement, a shifting of the ground. . . . The hard earth bulged again, and once more, and then there slowly emerged another monstrous greenish-brown egg. It rested immobile for a moment before it slowly, slowly began to move, drawing its ropy tail out of the hole behind it. Gam Lutie held her breath as it got nearer to Glocken, but it crawled round him and headed directly for the baby Digger.

She let it get right up to the wounded leg before she brought the sword down. The thing died without sound and with only a twitch of its long tail.

Swaying over the two collapsed egg-shapes, Gam Lutie tried to think. The things had ignored Glocken, but had gone for the baby Digger's injured leg. What had called them forth from the ground? The smell of blood? Or simply the break of day? Or . . . ? Her eyes fell on the still-smouldering campfire, and she rubbed her forehead tiredly. Whatever had brought them forth, they traveled round Glocken to reach the baby Digger. The baby Digger's wounded leg. Did they only attack the injured, then? Were you safe from them as long as you had no open wounds?

Scumble! Scumble had a hundred open wounds where the thorns had pierced his skin!

Scooping the baby Digger into her arms, she fled toward the spot where she had left Scumble. She paused to look at Silky, unharmed and peacefully asleep. But what she saw near the smoking ashes of the fire she had made there, sent her lurching, staggering on. Pits—half a hundred pits in the ground where there had been none before—and from each of them an ominous tail stretched like a thin snake. They were all going in the same direction. Toward Scumble.

The baby Digger whimpered and struggled in her arms, but she only held him tighter. She must hang on to him above all things, for it might be that she would have to use him to draw the egg-shapes away from Scumble.

The next moment, she was amongst them. The ground tilted and swayed with the army of murderous eggs. There was no mercy in Gam Lutie's sword as it hacked a way through the swarm to reach Scumble just beyond. The sword leaped in her hand, struck, and leaped again.

At last she was leaning over Scumble. None of the egg-shapes had reached him. Gam Lutie squeezed her eyes tight shut for an instant and drew a deep breath. She dared not think what would have happened had she lighted a fire near Scumble, for it was surely the heat of the fires which had drawn the egg-shapes from their beds to the attack. Had there been a fire closer than Silky's, the things could have broken ground and torn Scumble to shreds before she even knew of their existence. She wouldn't allow herself to think of Crustabread helpless somewhere on the desert. . . .

Turning abruptly, she waited for the rest of the egg-shapes to arrive. They paid no attention to their slain kin but moved over and round them to reach their own doom by the sword of the Minnipins. They came and came and came, and at last they came no more.

Stupid with fatigue, Gam Lutie let her sword tip touch the ground, its hilt once more cool in her palm. The dun earth was white with the thick substance that leaked from the egg-shapes, and she stepped back, sickened. Her mind was clotted with weariness and worry, but there was still so much to do. There was Crustabread. . . .

She called his name, feebly, hopelessly, knowing that he would not answer. The sky was flushed with color now. The sun, their enemy, had risen beyond the Barrier. When it topped the ridge, its full glare would sap her remaining strength. What must be done, must be done before the sun looked over the ridge.

She dropped to her knees beside Scumble and laid the baby Digger carefully on the ground. He made a soft whining noise, his eyes glazed with fear.

"It's all right," she said impatiently. The sound of her voice was strange after such a long silence—and oddly comforting. She went on talking, though of course the creature could have no idea of what she was saying. "We've got to get these thorns out of the way first. If the poison comes through the thorns, and Scumble so weakened already with the food poison. . . . And there is no more of the salve Muggles gave us. . . ."

The baby Digger lay watching her attentively, his greeny eyes wide and questioning.

Gam Lutie paused to pick a thorn from her own finger. The blood welled out. "If I had the salve," she went on, "I would put some on your leg too. I owe you that much, because if it hadn't been for your scream, the egg-shapes would have got Scumble before I knew they existed. Here, what are you trying to do? Lie still or you'll hurt your leg."

But the creature struggled to sit up, and seeing his determination, Gam Lutie stopped plucking thorns long enough to help him. He made peculiar little clicking sounds, and the greeny eyes bored into hers as though he would make her see into his mind. She nodded her head.

"Yes, yes, it's going to be all right."

The clicking came faster, and now he pointed at the cloven shells of the egg-shapes that lay behind her. Gam Lutie looked back fearfully, but nothing moved there.

"Yes, yes," she said irritably. "If any more of them come, I'll get rid of them." She put her hand to the hilt of the sword. It remained cool to her touch.

But now the baby Digger was pointing his needle-finger at her scratched and bloody hand, and his clicking cascaded over her. The finger swung back to the egg-shape, then once again to the scratches.

"What . . . ?" Gam Lutie sat back on her heels. "What are you trying to tell me? That the egg-shapes will come when they sense the blood? Yes, yes, I know that. I shall just—"

Scumble suddenly started thrashing about. Gam Lutie forgot the creature. She pulled and tugged Scumble upright and finally held his head while he got rid of the poisons in his stomach. Then she half-led, half-carried him a little distance away and lowered him to the ground between two of the poison-plants. He tried to say something to her, but his voice was the merest husk.

"It's all right," Gam Lutie said, hoping that it was. "Your throat is numb from the medicine, but it will pass. And you're stuck up with thorns, but I've got most of them out. Just go to sleep. I'll tuck you up." She pulled his cloak about him, wondering if Silky and Glocken were still covered. But dare she leave Scumble as long as there was danger of more egg-shapes appearing?

She went back to the spot where she had left the baby Digger. He wasn't there! She looked round frantically.

He was stretched out amongst the cloven shells, scooping up some of the thick white substance, which had flowed from them when the sword struck them in two. The thick white substance . . .

And then she knew! Knew what the little creature—the Wafer—had been trying to tell her.

She had found the source of the Mushrooms' marvelous healing salve!

9

And when the Minnipins had come safely through the tunnel in Frostbite, there were a many injured and weak. These were left at the water gap to recover and the Gam Lutie of Then did stay at the same place to nurse and comfort the infirm. Heroic of Heart, she bade her brother the Great Gammage farewell, for never would she see him nor indeed any folk but her charges from that moment henceforth. In time the Gam Lutie of Then chose a spouse from the recovered ones. . . .

—Walter the Earl, *Glorious True Facts in the History of the Minnipins from the Beginning to the Year of Gammage 880*

Minutes before, her very toes had been empty of force, but the discovery of the Mushrooms' precious ointment shot life back into Gam Lutie. It was possible that they might all die here under the enemy sun, but until that moment came, like that first Gam Lutie of Water Gap, she would do what had to be done.

The first act must be to repay her debt to the baby Digger—the Wafer, she reminded herself. It was only fitting that a creature who had perhaps saved their lives should be called by name. Stripping the bandages from his leg, she plastered the wounds with the thick salve scooped from the shells of the egg-shapes. Then she carried him to Scumble's side and made him as comfortable as possible on her own cloak. Scumble had so many scratches and punctures of the skin that she smeared a heavy coating of salve over most of him.

Anxious as she was to fetch Glocken and Silky, she first filled several of the split shells with the white substance and set them aside. A thin skin began forming over the top to seal the salve in. The sword was cold in her hand, and it remained cold as she traced the lifeless tails back to Silky's fire. The bush had completely burned out. Silky was sleeping, so she went on to Glocken. He, too, was asleep.

Gam Lutie found the moon-melon where it had rolled from the hamper and put it back. Beside it she stacked the water bottles that had been around the fire.

Glocken stirred. "Wh-what . . . ?"

"Glocken, are you all right?" She found four packs and piled them beside the hamper.

"I'm feeling hungry," he said thoughtfully. He raised himself with a groan on one elbow. "Hollow."

"Can you walk?"

Glocken struggled to get up and then sank back with a grunt. "Somebody's put water in my legs."

"I'll come back to help you," she promised, struggling into her own pack and picking up another and the hamper. "Don't wander off."

Glocken managed a sickly grin. "The only thing about me that could possibly wander is my mind. Where is everybody?"

She nodded in the general direction of the others. "And Glocken. . . . Keep your sword ready. If it grows warm, look out for a shell-creature like a great egg."

"An egg," he said wistfully. "Boiled or baked, it matters not. I might even fancy a raw one if the fire has gone out."

Gam Lutie stopped short. She didn't like silliness at any time, but to make a joke about eggs just now—her composure suddenly vanished. "If you can make quips at a time like this," she snapped, "you can bring yourself without my help. Scumble lies near death, and Crustabread is surely already dead somewhere I know not."

Her outburst gave new power to her legs, and she stalked off, closing her ears to Glocken's startled exclamations.

It was witless to fly at Glocken like that, she told herself as she at last dropped the hamper and the packs at the new campsite. The first Gam Lutie had never done such a thing. For just an instant, Gam Lutie wondered if that first one might not have lost her temper at some point or other without its getting into the history of the time. . . . She quickly dismissed the thought as disloyal and went back to fetch Silky.

Tea. Hot herb tea. They all needed it. But if she lit a fire, would it bring forth more of the egg-shapes? Why not? Bring them forth now and destroy them so that they couldn't come out later when she was busy at something else and perhaps unable to defend the camp.

She must rig a shelter of sorts. And Crustabread—she dared not think of the lost Crustabread. Get Silky . . . make tea . . . destroy eggshapes . . . rig shelter . . . make Silky get tea . . . no, no—

A sound froze her. She had just reached Silky and was bending over her when she heard it—a heavy, dragging sound. She snapped the sword from her side and wheeled to face this new threat.

A great humped monster was crawling toward her, its back undulating with the movement. She raised the sword high.

"Me," a weak voice said.

Gam Lutie let her arm fall nervelessly to her side. It was Glocken. He had the remaining two packs hitched over his shoulders, and his cloak, which was anchored to them, billowed as he crawled.

"Carry on," he said in a faint voice. "I'll be there . . . in time . . . for tea. . . ."

Tears of relief sprang to Gam Lutie's burning eyes, and she felt a sob rise in her dry throat. Somehow she hoisted Silky to her feet and started walking and carrying her to the others. Silky's head lolled back, and her legs scarcely worked at all. Gam Lutie had to drag her the last few yards.

There was no time to rest, for the sky over the Barrier was already the color of Prize the Baker's oven when it was ready for the loaves. Gam Lutie kindled a fire from one of the dry bushes and put a stone bottle to heat, keeping one hand on her sword, ready to strike at the first sign of an egg-shape.

But the sword remained cold and black, and the water finally boiled. She sprinkled in a liberal amount of sassafras and willow and set the flask to steep near the burning bush. When she judged the potion strong enough, she took it to her patients. By dint of coaxing and threatening, she fed some of the herb tea to Silky and Scumble and to the Wafer as well. Just as she began to worry about Glocken, she heard his slow, dragging crawl.

"Over here," she croaked through dry lips. "Your tea is ready."

She had to hold the steaming flask to his mouth, but he gulped the strong brew greedily.

When he stopped for air, he gasped, "What happened to us?"

"Fishcakes." Gam Lutie allowed herself the tiniest sip of the potion to wet her throat. She must save the rest for the sick. "I didn't eat any."

"You said about Crustabread?"

Gam Lutie shook her head hopelessly.

Was there a stirring there—just beyond the fire? Gam Lutie tightened her grip on the sword, felt it warm in her palm. The hard crust of earth shivered, cracked, and broke open in a dozen places.

Dizzily, Gam Lutie pushed herself up, felt the world recede from her in a whirling blackness. . . . *I must not*, she thought desperately, *I . . . must . . . not*. . . . She thrust at the nearest egg-shape, felt the sword leap downward once, and again and again and again until the hilt cooled in her hand. Only then did she sink trembling to the ground.

"Here." Glocken's voice was suddenly in her ear. She could smell it before she saw it, the overripe, repellent pulp of the moon-melon. When she made no move to take the piece, he shoved an end into her mouth. The juice ran cooling down her throat, and she was suddenly ravenous for more. Glocken clumsily hacked another piece out of the melon with his sword, and then another, until she signed to him to hold his hand.

She struggled to her feet. The sun was just showing over the Barrier, and already it seared the top of her head. "Eat," she commanded. "Then come." She wavered away from him to the spot where she had collected her patients.

The cloaks, light as milkweed on a Minnipin's shoulders, felt leaden in her hands as she spread them from bush to bush over Silky and Scumble and the Wafer. Somewhere in the desert around them lay Crustabread, with no cloak over him to filter out the sun.

She had just snagged the last cloak into place when she heard Glocken's slow crawl behind her.

"Don't know how . . . snakes manage," he gasped, pulling himself under the shade she had created. His eyes closed.

Slicing the rest of the moon-melon with her sword, she forced bits of the pulp into each of her patients. It was all she could do for them. Scumble's punctures were healing fast under the application of the white salve, and the Wafer's leg looked slightly better. Silky's breathing had lost its stutter. All of them slept.

Gam Lutie cut a slice of the moon-melon for herself and one for Crustabread. She found her pack and emptied it on the ground, refilling it with only the things she might need —Essence of Emptie, water-flask, herbs, firemakers. After a small hesitation, she added Muggles' *Maxims*. She didn't expect any help from the book, but in an unaccountable way, it was like having a friend with her. She had never had a friend before. Gam Luties didn't. *They* had villages. . . .

She put Glocken's sword into his hand and curled his fingers round the hilt. He seemed to understand, even in his exhausted sleep, and tightened his grasp. Last of all, she covered all of her cuts and scratches with the white salve. Then, taking out her own sword, she set off under the burning sun to find Crustabread.

The desert shimmered under her eyes and sometimes tilted

alarmingly, but she plodded on and on in ever-widening circles from the camp.

When she saw the brown woven slipper, she almost walked past it before her exhausted mind took it in. Even so, she stared down at it for moments without recognition. Then with a little cry, she dropped to her knees and tremblingly lifted it from the ground.

Crustabread's slipper. Discarded here in the empty desert, far from the camp, in the direction from which they had come. What did it mean? Gam Lutie sat back on her heels and gazed along the weary distance they had traveled from the tunnel's mouth. The mountains leaned toward her, but she knew it was only her eyes playing tricks. Then the ground in front of her heaved and buckled. More tricks. She ought to get up and go on. On where? The ground heaved again, bulged upward. It couldn't be egg-shapes. There was no fire here to bring them out of the ground.

And still the hard crust bulged and split— The answer struck her like a rush of wind. How could she have been so witless! She, Gam Lutie, of all folk, had become no more heedful than Silky. It was the *heat* of the fire that had brought forth the egg-shapes in the early light. And now there was another kind of heat—the heat of this desert sun.

She tried to get up, but her legs would no longer lift her. An egg-shape broke out of the crust a finger's length from her right hand. For a moment it stayed motionless, as though soaking up strength from the sun.

But it's not a creature, Gam Lutie thought in amazement. *It's a sort of plant, a fast-creeping plant.* But its tail? *Stem*, she corrected herself wonderingly. *Like a wild grapevine.*

Whatever it was, the egg-shape began creeping toward her left hand.

Powerless to move, Gam Lutie watched its slow advance. Surely it wouldn't attack her. She had smeared white salve on punctures, and they were already healing shut. Then she saw what had drawn the egg-shape. A long red, raw scratch stretched from her palm to the end of her thumb.

All around her the ground was bumping up now, but Gam Lutie was hardly aware of it. As the first of the creatures reached her hand and she felt its sharp tearing claws sink into her thumb, she found from somewhere the strength to raise the sword of the Minnipins in her other hand and cleave the shell in two. Then she plunged the injured hand into the oozing white substance. The sword slipped from her grasp and in reaching for it, her fingers closed over Crustabread's slipper instead.

She wondered what the book of *Maxims* would say now, had she the power to get it out of her pack. Probably it would give her hints for cooking cabbage— *When the pot boils dry, take it off the fire*. She felt a small smile working at her lips.

Well, she, Gam Lutie, had a maxim: *When the final task is done, it is time to sleep*.

Her last conscious thought was of Crustabread. Now she would never know what had become of him.

10

Jiggity, jiggity,
Jog along,
Jiggle the carts
With a Jostle-song.

Jiggery, jiggery,
Jolt away,
Jet your cares,
It's Jostle-Day.

—Traditional Song, for the Jostle-
races held every spring

It was a dream and yet not a dream. The painful jolting was real enough, but jostle-races had never been this bump-ity! Had the streets of Water Gap been torn up so badly then by the winter? But wait! How could the jostle carts go straight up in the air? And for that matter, how had she got into a jostle cart? She hadn't ridden in one since she was a child! Something was terribly wrong. She ought to stop the race at once—this was far too dangerous.

She slowly became aware that she was holding something tightly in her hand. But why did she feel this sense of loss when she looked at it? It was only a slipper, a rather badly worn slipper, somehow familiar. . . .

She closed her aching eyes. There was an overpowering smell of dust now—sun-warmed dust—that got into her nose and made her want to sneeze.

The next time she opened her eyes, all thoughts of jostle carts were gone, though the jolting and bouncing continued. Her head throbbed, and her eyes felt like burned-out pits, her throat like the dried scales of a trout. She turned her head as best she could—she seemed to be swaddled in something—and what she saw was so terrifying that she closed her eyes tight and looked no more. She was being hauled up the very face of the mountains on the back of a—Digger! And all around her, the sheer ascent was aswarm with Diggers! They climbed and clambered, finding finger- and toeholds where there were none.

Captured? Or saved? And where were the others? Were they too being carried, tied somehow to the backs of the Diggers? Terrified, she clung to the slipper as the only known object in a world of the unknown.

The swinging and jolting went on for what seemed like a lifetime, and then suddenly, she felt a change. True, she was still bobbing against the back of her Digger like a netful of trout slung over a fisherman's shoulder, but there was a difference. They were no longer climbing. She risked a glance.

She was on top of the world! There was nothing but sky everywhere she twisted her head. Sky, and a familiar humming—the sound of happy Diggers—all about her.

Then the motion stopped, and Gam Lutie swung helplessly in her cocoon—it was her own cloak that wrapped her round! The humming stopped too, and Gam Lutie had a horrifying thought. Was she to be stranded here on top of the world until some accident started the Diggers moving again?

Feebly she tapped the slipper on the head of her Digger in

an effort to make him move, but the next instant she regretted her action. The Digger gave a start, hesitated, and then brought his hand down on the head of his nearest neighbor with a force that felled him.

"Oh stop," Gam Lutie, cried, but it was too late. All around her, Diggers went down like reeds in a storm, humming and buzzing with delight, delivering blows with happy abandon before they themselves fell, then leaping up to play the game all over again.

But somewhere up ahead, a voice as low and carrying as a hooter-bird at dusk commanded, "Go, Diggers. Go, Diggers. Go, Diggers. Go." As the Diggers surged forward, Gam Lutie forgot her fears, the overpowering heat of the sun, the aches of her whole body.

The most beautiful sound in the whole world was that voice of the hooter-bird, for it belonged to Crustabread.

The Diggers' idea of descending a steep mountain slope seemed to be to drop three body lengths, touch rock for luck, and drop three more. Gam Lutie hung on to the slipper as though it were a magic rope suspended from the sky itself. Down they plummeted, down, down the endless mountainside. They were in shadow now, the sun hidden from them by the bulk of the mountain. And still they dropped through an eternity of time. Gam Lutie's head began to spin. It went round faster and faster until between one spin and the next, the sky, the side of the mountain, the smell of sun-warmed dust—all became one great whirl.

First there was the noisome smell. Then something cool and moist and sweet went trickling down her throat. Gam

Lutie swallowed gratefully, and kept on swallowing as more of the liquid followed. The ground seemed to rock beneath her, but it *was* the ground she was half-sitting, half-lying on. And whoever was holding her up wasn't a Digger. After a while she opened her eyes.

"Ng . . . that's better." Crustabread's face above hers was creased in anxious lines. He poured some more of the juice from a moon-melon shell into her mouth and almost choked her.

"Oh Crustabread," she spluttered. "I thought you were dead."

"Ng . . . I'm not. Sit up and eat this." He thrust a big chunk of juicy melon into her hand and pushed her upright. "Do you see that?"

Bewildered by the violent changes of this day, Gam Lutie took some time to sort out what Crustabread was showing her. They were on the other side of the Barrier, shaded from the westering sun by the great rock bulk. The shadow ended abruptly a short distance from them as though somebody had drawn a line, and the sunlit desert stretched beyond and beyond. But as she looked, it moved and shifted and moved again.

"Diggers?" she asked.

"They're getting restless," said Crustabread. "They don't like this side of the Barrier." He pointed along the line of shadow toward the south. "Our folk are just beyond those two big rocks. We'll start off as soon as you've eaten. Before the Diggers start off without us." He stood up and walked away, came back. "Could I have my slipper now?"

Gam Lutie released the slipper from her cramped hand,

watched him put it on. "You brought the Diggers, didn't you?" she asked suddenly.

He jerked his head.

"And you lost your slipper on the way? And couldn't find it because it was still dark when you left?"

Another jerk of the head.

"Then you didn't eat any of the fishcakes?"

A faint smile touched his serious mouth. "I've never fancied left-over food."

"Crustabread. . . ."

He stamped his foot in the slipper. "There, that's better." He gave her a sidelong look. "Ng . . . it—it was a kind thought to come looking for me. If that's what you were doing so far from the others?"

"Why yes. I—"

"I found your cloak where you had left it. The Wafer was asleep on it." Crustabread's tone was gruff, but Gam Lutie suddenly realized that he was trying to say thank you for all of them.

She looked after his retreating figure wonderingly. He must have started back for the Diggers the moment Glocken went down with the sickness, for he hadn't even taken off his pack. He knew what was going to happen before it happened, and he didn't lose any time in discussion. He simply went. And somehow he had got the Diggers on the move, got them to carry the Minnipins over the Barrier on their untiring backs. . . .

And now . . . Gam Lutie's eyes swept over the desert before them and came to rest on the mountain towering up to the sky to the left of her. It had a familiar, yet not-quite-familiar look. Munching on the moon-melon, she puzzled over this until suddenly she realized what she was gazing at, and she felt a tingling at the back of her neck, for the mountain was ancient Frostbite. A Frostbite seen in reverse, like— she felt a sudden thrill of excitement—like the Whisper Stone! Beyond its crags lay the Land Between the Mountains. And the village of Water Gap—under water.

She pushed herself on to her stiff legs and began walking as fast as she could in the direction Crustabread had taken.

They were all there, on the other side of the two large rocks. Scumble leaned feebly against one of the boulders, limp as a dummy from a Haggle fete, the Wafer asleep between him and a pile of moon-melons. Silky and Glocken were at work over the shoulder packs, sorting out the jumble of water bottles, while Crustabread watched the Diggers under the visor of his hand.

"I don't begin to understand all that happened," Silky was saying, "but from the tangle everything is in, Gam Lutie must have thought it was house-cleaning time."

"Gam Lutie," said Crustabread without looking round, "saved all your lives."

"I thought *you* did that," said Silky, "by going after the Diggers."

"And before that," said Glocken, "it was Scumble bringing the moon-melons."

"And before *that*," said Silky, "Glocken made the Diggers fill up the pit so that we could get out. I suppose," she added somewhat glumly, "that makes everybody a hero except me."

Scumble tried to say something, but no sound came out.

Gam Lutie hurried forward. "It's the Essence that has taken your voice," she explained. "I gave it to you full strength."

Silky looked up with a gasp. "But you *knew* you shouldn't!" she cried indignantly. "It says right on the bottle —we *talked* about it."

Scumble waved a silencing hand before Gam Lutie could get her mouth unstuck. He pointed to Silky and then cradled his arms as though rocking a baby.

"What is he getting at?" asked Glocken.

Gam Lutie shrugged. If Scumble wanted to say that Silky's care of the little Wafer had brought the friendship of the Diggers and so she was a hero too, he could tell her at such time as he got his voice back. She, Gam Lutie, wasn't going to say it for him.

Silky pulled a half-shell out of the pack she was sorting. "I wonder where this came from," she mused, poking a cautious finger at the dried white crust that sealed the half-shell. "Poisonous looking," she announced in disgust and raised her arm to fling the precious salve into the distance.

"No!" Gam Lutie shouted.

Silky dropped the half-shell in fright, and it clattered along the hard ground. Gam Lutie stumbled after it. Luckily, it hadn't cracked, but the hard crust was dislodged, and precious ointment oozed out.

"Well!" said Silky.

It was several moments before Gam Lutie could find her voice. It came out hard and cold. "You are silly and unthinking and unfit to be on an expedition of this nature. These shells contain the magic salve of the Mushrooms, and it is fortunate for all of us that Crustabread had the brain not to leave them behind when he found us. But you with your carelessness were about to fling away the very thing that may mean life instead of death for us all."

"Oh!" Silky brought her foot down hard in her fury. "How could I *know!* And when it comes to flinging precious salve away, I seem to remember . . ."

Scumble made scraping noises in his throat and motioned violently from one to the other.

"He says," Glocken guessed, "that both of you should save your quarrel until we're back in Water Gap."

"Oh, all right," said Silky grudgingly. "I'm glad you found the salve, Gam Lutie, and thank you for saving our lives, and I may not be very useful. . . ."

"That is true," Gam Lutie replied. She still felt cold with anger at Silky's flitter-wing nature, but she forced herself to give a gracious nod. "However, you are forgiven."

Crustabread broke the stiff silence that followed. "We can't rest any longer," he announced. "The Diggers are beginning to break up."

Her lips pressed tightly together, Gam Lutie stowed the shells of ointment safely away in the herb basket. Silky shrugged and busied herself tearing a strip from the hem of her brown-weave dress and fashioning a sling with which she could carry the baby Digger. Scumble sliced up a moon-melon, and Glocken distributed the pieces amongst the packs.

Meanwhile, Crustabread had joined the Diggers, his sand cloak vanishing like magic into the restless blend of Digger and desert. When long minutes crept by and nothing happened, Gam Lutie went out into the sunglare after him.

She found the Diggers gathered round Crustabread and

Master Mayor, who had their hands intertwined like a game of Carry-All. Sweat poured down Crustabread's face as he coaxed and cajoled and harangued the puzzled Diggers.

"Come on. One of you. Sit. Sit on our hands." But the Diggers only twined arms and hands with each other in mime of what they saw.

"No, no," cried Crustabread. "Sit! Like this!" He made as if to sit, and immediately all the Diggers began bobbing up and down like corks. And as they bobbed, a humming rose. . . .

Crustabread caught sight of Gam Lutie as she pushed her way through the buzzing throng. "Here!" he cried. "Gam Lutie, show them how to sit on a Carry-All. Owwww!" One of Master Mayor's fingerpoints had accidentally raked his arm, and blood welled in the scratch. "Careful of their spikes."

Gam Lutie gingerly sat herself in the Carry-All made by Crustabread's and Master Mayor's wrist-grips.

"Now. . . . Go, Diggers. Go, Diggers. . . ." The Carry-All moved toward the shadow beneath the Barrier where the other Minnipins waited.

Instantly all was pandemonium as the Diggers broke their wrist-grips on each other to become sitters, only to discover that there were no Carry-Alls left to sit on. They re-formed, broke apart, re-formed once more, all with an urgent bleating, until at last they somehow stumbled into a solution of the problem. The bleating turned into humming as the Carry-Alls, each with a rider, loped sidewards toward the base of the Barrier.

Here there was more confusion as Crustabread wheedled and scolded the Diggers into dumping their riders and taking on new ones. There was further delay while he convinced Master Mayor that the Digger must have a new partner and let Crustabread ride.

But at last the Minnipins were all mounted on the Carry-Alls, the go-word was given, and the Diggers took off across the desert, veering left toward Frostbite.

Gam Lutie's bones had been rattled about so much since the moment they had been catapulted out of the tunnel into the pit that she found the present jouncing and jolting easy enough—once she had overcome her reluctance to clutch those thin powdery arms that held her. Actually there was something reassuring in the sun-warmed scent of the Diggers, and their happy buzz meant that all was well. If it weren't for the penetrating heat and a vague uneasiness of mind over her sharp words to Silky. . . . *Nonsense*, she thought, *a Gam Lutie must be above having feelings. Feelings are just what is wrong with Silky.*

Gradually she became aware of a sound that had been growing in the air for some little time—a sort of dull whine that was a background to the happy buzz of the Diggers. Had their humming grown less hummy in the last few minutes, or was that her imagination? It seemed to her, too, that her Carry-All's pace had slackened.

They *had* slowed down. Gam Lutie no longer bounced as she rode. She tightened her grip on the bearers' stringy arms. If they were afraid of what lay before them, these creatures who were so scattered of brain that they forgot everything, shouldn't the Minnipins beware?

Suddenly something flew past her head with a whistling sound. There was a shrill cry from behind her. Thin shrieks rose on all sides to join it.

Gam Lutie's seat disappeared from under her as her two bearers dropped hands and fled in the opposite direction—back toward the Barrier they had crossed. She fell sprawling, and a forest of spidery legs passed over and round her.

I must tell her, she thought. *I must tell Silky that it doesn't matter she's flittery.*

11

Big fish swallow little fish in the middle of a yawn.

—Muggles, *Further Maxims*

Glocken had just patted his heart pocket once more to be sure that the Whisper Stone hadn't bounced out when a long shaft whistled past his ear faster than a blink. Shrieks tore the air, the Carry-All in front of him collapsed, and Glocken went kiting into the air, all in a jumble of time. He landed in the midst of a churning mass of legs, which miraculously disappeared one moment later.

Cautiously, he raised his head. He could hardly see for the dust. That thing in the foreground looked like—he shut his eyes, then opened them to try again. But the picture did not vanish the way the legs had. It was one of the Diggers stretched flat on the ground with a wooden shaft sticking straight up from his chest. Beyond the dead Digger was a huddle of dusty sand. Glocken's heart tried to come up in his throat. He swallowed it down.

"Crustabread!" he called fearfully and was relieved to see the huddle of sand raise a head. Then other heads popped up above the low scrub. Gam Lutie . . . Scumble . . . Silky farther on. . . . As the dust raised by the wild flight of the Diggers slowly settled, Glocken felt his eyeballs stiffen. Advancing toward them on legs like tree trunks was the cause of the Diggers' panic.

Swathed in billowing white, with hats like overturned bread baskets topping their coarse faces, the great hulking creatures took squashing footsteps across the desert, heedless of what was crushed beneath. There were ten or twelve of them, measuring at the very least three Minnipins high. They carried in their hands huge machines shaped like crosses, and each cross held one of the long shafts like that sticking into the dead Digger.

Glocken shuddered. What would creatures like these care about Minnipins? No more than they cared about a band of Diggers. Those massive arms would crush a Minnipin with as little trouble as a Minnipin stepping on a cobbler beetle while crossing the market square.

And so they had come to the end of their adventure. . . . With sudden yearning Glocken longed to see his bell tower once more, to play the carillon during the long soft evenings of summer, even to feel the familiar ache of wanting to follow the Watercress River to its source, to pore over the old scrolls and dream again of one day making the name of Glocken sweet to Minnipin ears. And now—now he would never know what the Whisper Stone meant, whether it was a map of some sort, as Walter the Earl thought, or only a charm that had run out of good luck.

A shout like a crack of thunder jolted his head up. He froze, only his eyeballs twitching. The great things were still some distance away, and one of them was bending over. When he straightened, he held between his haunch-like hands a struggling figure, like an undersized child caught up from mischief-making.

With mounting anguish Glocken realized that the child was Silky. Her sheeny cloak aswirl, she was beating at the great thing's face and kicking at his stomach.

"Put me down! Put me down, you—you Hulk!"

There was more thunder—rolls of it—and flashes of white streaking across the big ugly faces. Glocken's hands crept toward the hilt of his sword. Why. . . . He blinked, forgetting about the sword. They were laughing! The huge coarse things were laughing and slapping themselves in a wild sort of glee. Then the one who was holding the struggling Silky hoisted her to his shoulder and boomed out something that made the others laugh all the more. Glocken's hand closed

on his sword. It took him moments to realize that it remained cold and lifeless to his touch! He clutched it tighter, as though to warm it from his own palm.

The merry-making came to a sudden end. A great roar swept across Glocken like a windblow. Another white figure was striding angrily across the desert toward the Hulk who held Silky.

"Put—it—down!"

Sullenly the Hulk obeyed, dumping Silky roughly on the ground.

Glocken blinked twice before he realized that he had actually understood the words. His heart gave a wild leap.

The sword remained cold, and these creatures talked like Minnipins.

As Silky indignantly shook out her cloak, the newcomer planted himself before her, arms folded.

"WE—ARE—FRIENDS. FRIENDS. WE—WON'T—HARM—YOU. FRIENDS. DO—YOU—UNDERSTAND? WE—ARE—FRIENDS. WE—WON'T—HARM—YOU.

"Then stop shouting," Silky cried. "You'll burst my ear-holes!"

The Hulk's mouth dropped open. "YOU—YOU SPEAK OUR TONGUE?"

"I should have said that *you* speak ours," Silky answered tartly.

"WHERE DO YOU . . ." the Hulk started, but when he saw Silky clap her hands over her ears, he quickly dropped his voice to a rumble, still too loud, but bearable. ". . . come from?"

It suddenly occurred to Glocken that a true hero didn't lurk behind a prickle bush when one of his folk was facing up to possible peril. Cautiously, he stood up and walked forward, hand on sword. Scumble bobbed up nearby, Gam Lutie farther off. Glocken had to go round two more felled Diggers, each stuck to the ground with one of the shafts.

The Hulks gaped, their shaft-machines forgotten as the Minnipins moved slowly toward them. Glocken could feel his knees quake as he got closer. The sword remained reassuringly cold, but it took a tremendous effort all the same not to turn and flee from these enormous folk with their cruel machines.

The leader stood staring down at the Minnipins as they

gathered about Silky. So close, he was even more terrifying. The hair that showed under the basket hat was the color of a wild red carrot, and the short coarse stubs of whiskers sprouting from his chin and upper lip were the same rusty orange. When he smiled, as he did suddenly, his teeth were like fences. Glocken shuddered.

One of the machine-holders stretched out his enormous hand toward Silky's head, but the watchful leader, frowning as suddenly as he had smiled, barked a sharp order. The hand whipped back as though it had been stung.

"He means no harm," explained the Red Carrot, showing his fencelike teeth again. Glocken wished he wouldn't. "We have never seen a people as small as you, though we have heard stories about such. You must forgive us if we have hurt your dignity by picking you up like a child."

"A child!" Silky burst out. "If that's the way you pick up your children, they must have bones of oak."

"We offer apologies," the Red Carrot said. "We have no wish to hurt you. Where is your land?"

Glocken cleared his throat. In all the stories and legends which had come down through the years, there was a spokesman. Being a spokesman was one thing Glocken knew all about. He stepped forward and removed his hat with a sweep, but when the sun hit his head like Nail the Carpenter's hammer, he clapped the hat on again.

"Know then"—he addressed the Hulks at the top of his lungs—"that we live in the valley beyond Frostbite . . ." and he waved his hand toward the mountain. "We lived in peace until the Watercress River, the very lifeline of our valley, flooded our village and we had to flee." Here, Glocken's eloquence deserted him, and he glared accusingly at the Red Carrot. "Our whole village flooded out, and the next village too. Everybody had to leave. We lost our homes, our clothing, our food, our belongings. And now. We came in peace to learn what happened to our river. We came in peace and were met by stickers."

"Stickers?"

Glocken motioned impatiently at one of the fallen Diggers. "Whatever that is you stuck them with." He gave a snort. "*Friends* you call yourselves!"

"But those—" The Red Carrot waved a contemptuous hand toward the dead Digger. "It's the only way to keep the pests from destroying our years of work. They don't understand anything but force." He dismissed the whole race of Diggers with a shrug. "You need rest and food. My guards will carry you to the camp."

"Thank you." Gam Lutie spoke up with ice in her voice. "I for one prefer to carry myself."

The Red Carrot looked fixedly at her. "See here," he said, his voice getting louder, "it's TOO FAR. YOU LOOK—sorry!—worn out. My guards will carry you."

One moment they were standing on the ground, and the next, the Minnipins were whisked upward by strong arms. Before any of them could protest, they were off across the sandy waste, held firmly on the shoulders of the Stickermen.

Glocken wrinkled his nose and gulped hard. How strong these folk smelled!—not at all like the rather pleasant sun-washed dusty scent of the Diggers, but sharp and acid and rank like the leaf of the skink-root when crushed underfoot. And their faces sprouted stubby hair in pores like ditches. Glocken gave a shudder of dismay. Folk so large and coarse couldn't help but smash little things, no matter how friendly they thought themselves. They were big, and they lived big.

For a long time—perhaps even before the Diggers had dumped them on the ground—Glocken had been aware of a new sound going on somewhere behind all the near-at-hand sounds, but now, as they came closer to the mountain, the sound grew louder. Keeping his nose pinched together against the overpowering smell of the Stickerman, Glocken stared intently at the forbidding reaches of Frostbite, which they were fast approaching. There could be no doubt now that the Whisper Stone showed the outline of this mountain with its two spurs jutting out into the desert. But what of the markings on the Stone? In vain Glocken scanned the face of the mountain. Nothing there corresponded to the markings. But there was something else. Joining the two spurs and extending from the bottom high up the mountain was a dazzling white Apron. The ground at the base of the Apron whirled with activity, like an anthill that had been muddled with a stick.

Glocken squinted fiercely to filter out the sundazzle. At regular intervals something flew through the air past the white Apron and disappeared from view into the desert. And the anthill. . . . Weren't those houses that stretched out in precise rows from the white Apron? Was it only another trick of the heat haze that made them seem to billow and flap as though they had a life of their own?

The party speeded its pace now, and Glocken had all he could do to keep his seat on the broad shoulder. The wind made by their rapid motion, though cooling, threatened to blow him away. Furthermore, great globs of water kept trickling down the Hulk's neck into his loose shirt so that soon Glocken was sitting in a pool of water. Bracing himself

against the basket hat, Glocken leaned down to the big ugly ear.

"Heigh! How do you call yourself?"

The Hulk made no response.

Experimentally, Glocken blew at the hairs that stood like trees in the porch of his ear. The tops of the stalks wavered slightly.

Glocken considered. These beings were deaf to small sounds. When you were being carried off to an unknown place by great Hulks, it was well to note any weaknesses you could find.

Cupping his hand against the wind, Glocken yelled into the tremendous whorl. "Have you got a name?"

The massive head turned, and Glocken shrank back from the red-veined eye which blinked at him.

"You said?"

Glocken abated his voice. "What's your name?"

The heavy eyelid dropped over the bulging eye like a sluice gate coming down and then traveled slowly upward.

"Nine," he said. "Just call me Nine." And he tapped the front of his basket hat with a clonk that almost sent Glocken flying. Then he saw that the number nine was painted on it. It seemed an odd way to name folk. How could you get to know somebody called Number Nine?

The head turned to the front once more, and Glocken gave up asking about the white Apron on the mountain and the flying things and the houses that flapped. Besides, so fast did the Hulks cover ground with their long legs that they were almost up to the mountainside and had indeed come to the outer fringe of the—they were houses, certainly, but

Glocken gaped at them in astonishment, for they were made of cloth!

A moment later they were running along a wide path between the flapping houses, and he could see inside them. They seemed badly furnished—a cot and a chest. Some of the houses were being pulled down and rolled into packs, and here and there stood huge wheeled carts to receive the packs.

A Hulk suddenly let out a yell as they passed, and then there were more shouts and the pounding of feet in pursuit of the Stickermen with their burden of Minnipins. The Stickermen merely put on more speed and easily outdistanced the others. More and more of the rolled-up houses were being stowed in the carts. There were sky-shaking shouts and earth-trembling stampings about. Through it all ran the unmistakable bustle, though more like a stampede in this case, of departure.

Then a shadow like that of a giant bird passed over them, and Glocken forgot all else. It was one of the carts, complete with wheels, riding through the air! This was a magic that made puny the swords of the Minnipins! Another cart whined past, bucketing a little with its speed, and then a third, coming from the other direction. By the time the fourth came along, Glocken saw that it wasn't the wheels bearing the carts through the air—they were only idly turning with the motion—but two metal cords that extended as far as he could see. The carts were strung on the cords like buckets in a well! Stickerman Nine paid no attention to the flying carts but went tirelessly slogging along.

The background noise had turned into an insistent hum—not like the happy buzz of the Diggers, but nagging, discordant. As they got nearer to the white Apron of the mountain, the hum grew more piercing, interrupted by an intermittent jangling that made Glocken clench his teeth. His head had begun to thump with all the noise and confusion. Another cart bucketed overhead, and close behind it still another. The jangling grew into a clashing, until Glocken thought his brain would turn to mince.

Just as the noise became unendurable, the Stickermen turned away from it. Only when they had got well past, did Glocken realize what he had seen. There was a platform and a ramp and some giant gear-like machinery to which the whining-cords were attached. Around these things swarmed a great number of Hulks in their white flowing garments. Some were hooking a loaded cart on to the whining-cord; others were pushing new carts up the incline to take its place. It was a loading platform for the flying carts!

Then they entered a large square that ran the length of the vast Apron now towering over them. They seemed to be heading for a tower that was built right into the center of the Apron. Hulks were clumping everywhere on their log-like legs, but only a few, eyeballs bulging, stopped to stare. The little party had almost reached the tall white tower when one of the Hulks suddenly shouted:

"They're not childer! They're full-grown!"

All motion in the vicinity of the Minnipins stopped, and there was a rolling "Ah-h-h-h"—of astonishment, of curiosity, of delight, of disbelief. Then the crowd surged. From all over the square white-clothed Hulks converged to see the Little Ones. From where Glocken sat, it looked like hundreds of bobbing baskets on a river—noisy baskets. He hung on to Number Nine's hat with all his might.

The Red Carrot shouted, "Stay back, stay back!" but he might as well have puffed at the north wind. Hulks stuck their broad faces directly into the Minnipins' faces and laughed braying laughs that deafened them. Someone snatched Glocken's shoe and his hat, and he saw a sky-blue ribbon fluttering in an ugly haunch of a hand—it was Silky's sash. Gam Lutie's hat spun on a thick finger, and Glocken's heart sank. It was unthinkable that anyone should violate Gam Lutie's person in any way. Helplessly, he put his hand to his sword. What was wrong with it? Didn't it know they were in danger of being torn limb from limb?

And then the Red Carrot blew a blast on a whistle. It was a sound to drive the senses from one's head. Glocken, half-deafened and reeling from the shock, clung to Number Nine's hat. This was a powerful weapon, he thought with dismay. Another blast. He could only hang on. But why did Number Nine not flinch from the sound? The other Hulks were hurrying off in the direction of the cloth houses that ringed the open space, leaving a few who still crowded about the Minnipins, snatching and clawing at their clothes. Somebody got hold of Glocken's cloak and pulled, almost choking the life from him. And then, suddenly, a door in the white tower flew open and erupted a series of dazzling flashes. Blinded as well as deafened, the Minnipins could only cling with their remaining strength to their captors.

There were cracks and thunks and groans and cries and sounds like that of moon-melons thrown on the ground. Hulks, clutching bloody heads or arms or shoulders, were shuffling or crawling or limping off to the cloth houses.

Glocken became dimly aware that the flashes came from silver helmets worn by Hulks with special red belts around their middles. They had wooden clubs in their hands with which they were laying about as though they enjoyed it. Glocken shuddered and closed his eyes again.

He lost track of events for a little while. He realized that they had gone inside and there had been strange lumpy food to eat, but his next clear thought arrived in the midst of a cloudburst. As the cool water exploded on his head, he turned to run, only to discover that he was in a small cloth room! Was there no end to the marvels of these Hulks? To produce a shower of rain indoors . . . his mind boggled.

After a while the rain stopped, and Glocken could see the source of it far above his head—holes punched in pipes that ran along the top of the room.

A huge hairy hand reached inside one of the cloth walls with an enormous length of towel. When Glocken, wrapped in it, emerged from the rain room, he found himself in another cloth room, empty except for an oversized stool on which lay some white garments. There was no sign of Glocken's own clothing. There was no sign of his sword. And . . . his heart sank . . . no sign of the Whisper Stone.

The garments proved to be shirt and breeches and a cloak roughly corresponding to his size but whacked crudely out of coarse cloth and sewed together with gigantic stitches. There were padded slippers of a sort. Glocken felt faintly ridiculous walking out of the room in clothing of such coarseness, but there seemed to be nothing else to do. He pulled aside one curtained wall but found that it led into another room exactly like the one he was already in. He tried another wall. This gave onto a vast expanse of hall which was divided and subdivided by curtains hung from a network of poles. Above them pipes snaked across the ceiling. It was one vast rain room!

The scraping of chair legs on the washed limestone floor made Glocken jump. But it was only Number Nine looming over him. The Stickerman motioned him to follow and led the way to a big door, his footsteps setting up a clattering echo that bounced off the ceiling at Glocken. He had to half-run to keep up.

They came out into a windowless corridor, chill and dim and damp, with more of the echoing, but there was a new sound here, that seemed to come from behind the inner wall of limestone. It was a thumping and a thrashing, as though ten reed mills were grinding at top speed all at once. A ladder led to a metal door set high up in the wall, and that was all there was to see in the corridor.

They went through another door, into blinding light. When Glocken could bear to open his eyes a squinch, he saw that he was in a room with huge windows looking out onto the square where the Hulks had snatched at them. There wasn't much in the room besides some chairs, a great flat table—and the Red Carrot. His hair was a frightening sight without the basket hat to subdue its effect. No Minnipin had ever had such hair.

"PLEASE SIT DOWN," the Red Carrot said, in a voice that bounced off the walls and hung jangling in the room.

Glocken looked at the available seats and decided he was too tired to climb into one of the huge chairs.

"I'll stand," he said.

The Red Carrot leaned over the table. "SPEAK UP!" he roared. The blast of his breath made Glocken's hair wave like grass in the wind.

Glocken had just got his own breath back when it was choked off again by an unexpected journey to the seat of a chair. Number Nine had taken matters into his own hands.

From the higher vantage point of the chair, Glocken could see what was lying on the table between him and the Carrot. Four swords. Four swords of the Minnipins, looking for all the world on that expanse like four old and blunt carving knives.

The Red Carrot was shouting something again, but Glocken was too unsettled by the sight of the swords in captivity to understand what he said. *Four* swords! Where was the fifth? He felt a little chill of excitement. One of them had managed to keep his sword hidden from the Hulks!

He raised his eyes from the tantalizing swords and found himself mirrored in the bulging eyeballs of the Carrot.

"Well," said that one, and for a wonder he had brought his voice down to a throaty rumble, like thunder leashed to far mountain peaks. "I find it hard to remember that your ears are so sensitive. I am almost whispering now. Can you hear me?"

Glocken nodded, trying to look away from the glistening eyeballs but unable to withdraw his gaze. They were crisscrossed with red veins like a network of paths, but what really held Glocken were the ice-blue pools in the center. He had the sudden feeling that he might drown in them.

"We intend to help you," the Carrot rumbled on. "We

are sorry that we have flooded your land, but we promise to repay you a thousandfold. I believe that your companions are already asleep, and I won't keep you long from your bed. I only want to ask you a question or two. Now I understand that you are called Minnipins and that you are fisherfolk and reed-growers and watercress-eaters, and that you set out from your home of Water Gap because the Watercress River has flooded your village. Is that correct?"

Glocken nodded. His head had begun to throb, and his stomach felt caved-in. The very mention of a bed made him overpoweringly sleepy. It was hard to keep his mind on what the Red Carrot was saying.

The ice-blue pools in the red-veined eyes went on bulging at him. "We are a friendly people, and nobody in distress has ever gone from us empty-handed. I can promise you that as soon as your plight is made known to my people, they will make full restitution and more."

Glocken nodded again and almost kept on going over with the weight of his head.

The Carrot rose with such a clatter that Glocken jerked wide awake. "I can see that you are exhausted," said the Carrot, "so I will come directly to my questions. The first concerns this book which was found in the pocket of the one called Gam Lutie." He drew the book of Muggles' *Maxims* from somewhere inside his voluminous garments and put it on the desk. "I should like to have it, but Gam Lutie said it belonged to all of you. Do you object to my keeping it?"

Glocken looked at him blankly, not sure he had understood.

The Carrot let the book fall open on the table. "I find the

sayings in here very pithy, and I should like to take them back to my country." He peered at the opened page, reading, and suddenly gave a chuckle that made Glocken start. "Listen to this: *Give carefully. Take even more carefully*. Very well. I shall pay this Muggles a suitable sum for her book of *Maxims* to avoid any trouble with give and take!"

He laughed loudly, and Glocken gave a feeble smile, though he only wished to be done with the Carrot and find a bed.

The Carrot suddenly became grave and leaned forward. "The other thing—is this!" He brought his hand up and smacked it down on the table, his eyes all the time fixing Glocken like a pin in a flitter-wing. After what seemed like a long time, he raised his hand to reveal—the Whisper Stone.

Glocken sucked in his breath.

"Well?" asked the Carrot. "What is it?"

Glocken hunted for his voice. "A—a charm."

"What is the Whisper of Glocken?"

"A bell, I think."

"Speak up, SPEAK UP," said the Carrot, following his own advice. Glocken winced.

"A bell," he said as loudly as his aching head would allow.

"A *bell!*" There was disbelief, exasperation, and a tinge of laughter in the Carrot's tone.

Glocken drew himself up. "Yes, a bell. I am a bell-ringer and my name is Glocken. The Whisper is a bell that belongs to my family. . . ." He wished he didn't feel so weak and sick; otherwise, he could have regaled the Carrot with the whole series of Pretends about the Whisper of Glocken.

". . . and the Whisper Stone is a charm handed down from the first Glocken to—"

"What are these scratchings? What do they mean?"

Glocken shrugged, all at once wary. He couldn't be sure why, but it seemed important not to let the Carrot know that the Whisper Stone might be a map. "You can see," he said carefully, "that it is Frostbite Mountain. At the bottom is the Watercress River flowing . . . er . . . *into* the tunnel. That's where our village is, but it's not in the picture. The Whisper . . . er . . . the Whisper hangs above the tunnel, and . . . and when the wind blows, the bell sounds like a whisper so that folk turn to each other in the square and say, 'Listen, do you hear the Whisper of Glocken?' " He was quite carried away by his invention and might have gone on in spite of his weariness if he weren't frightened by the way the Carrot's hand hovered possessively over the Whisper Stone. He wanted to get the Stone back before the Carrot realized that it showed the desert side, not the valley side, of Frostbite. He forced himself to keep his voice steady and unconcerned.

"I was afraid I had lost my charm," he said, holding out his hand. "Thank you for watching over it for me. It contains all the luck of the Glockens."

"Well. . . ." Reluctantly the Carrot inspected the Stone one last time and handed it over. "I was also interested in a small pouch containing gold coins," he added as though it was an afterthought.

There was something in those deep-blue pools that warned Glocken.

"I was just wondering," said the Carrot with infinite casualness, "how you got your gold. I suppose there are old mines . . . ?"

"Not *gold* mines," Glocken lied glibly. "The gold came from a place that none of us knows anything about save the name—Golden Mountain. The Minnipins once dwelt there, but they left during the dry time, that is 885 Gammage-years ago."

"I . . . see." The Carrot pursed his lips thoughtfully and leaned back to pull on a rope that hung down the wall behind him. A bell jangled outside the room.

It was Number Nine who came to take him away. Glocken was so near to collapse that he made no protest when the Stickerman swung him to his shoulder.

They mounted stone stairs then, up and around and around and up. Glocken caught sight of wide hallways opening off the stairway at intervals. They met Hulks on the steps. Hands reached out to poke and prod at him, as though he were some kind of curious fish hauled up in a net. One well-meant pat on the pate almost drove his head through his shoulders. He tried to protest, but his voice was lost in the great booming echoes of the stairwell.

When at last the stairs ended and they stopped before a huge door, Glocken felt broken in a dozen places. Another Stickerman, posted by the door, swung it open for them, and they passed into a chamber, dimly lighted by a small high window. There was a big table in the center of the room, some rock slabs against a wall, and a pile of white laundry in the corner. Number Nine swung him down on the laundry and drew a piece of it up to cover him.

Glocken just remembered thinking that the laundry

seemed to have faces mixed up in it, Minnipin faces; then he stopped thinking altogether.

But he seemed scarcely to have dropped into the blackness of sleep, when he jumped awake again. Every joint and every fiber of him ached. He cautiously turned his head—and found himself staring straight into Scumble's eyes! He must have made some sort of surprised noise because beyond Scumble another head popped up.

"He's awake!"

"Silky?" he said wonderingly. "It *is* you, isn't it? You look so queer in those clothes."

"Oh, Glocken," gasped Silky, "do you know anything about the Wafer? We don't have him. When the Diggers dropped us, he must have got out of the sling."

Glocken shook his head.

"It does no good to worry," said another voice. With dignity, Gam Lutie rose to her feet in the corner and shook and straightened her coarse white dress and cloak. "I told you yesterday, and I say it today, the Wafer has a better chance on the desert than here with these Hulks, who war on the Diggers."

"Yesterday!" Glocken exclaimed. "What do you mean about yesterday? We didn't even know the Hulks then."

Gam Lutie gave an exaggerated sigh. "Could somebody explain to Glocken that he's been asleep the clock round?"

He was so astonished that he got right up on his feet without feeling his aches and bruises. "Do you mean that it's now *tomorrow?*"

"That's right," said Silky with a little laugh. "And today is yesterday."

He *was* confused. And there was something else he was

156

confused about. Something that was amiss earlier today—no, yesterday—in the Red Carrot's room. Something that made him feel uneasy. . . .

"I see that they've seen fit to give our packs and the herb basket back to us," said Gam Lutie, walking over to the small heap beside the door. "But no swords."

Swords! That was it—the four Minnipin swords on the table in front of the Red Carrot. Four, not five. Confusedly, Glocken tried to remember the journey into the cloth city on the shoulder of Number Nine and, before that, the moments when they had stood in the desert confronting the Stickermen.

"What's wrong?" Silky demanded. "What's wrong with you, Glocken? You're not ill again?"

He heard her only dimly. The very last time he had seen Crustabread, then, was—the heap of sand stirring and becoming the sand-colored cloak. Just after the Diggers had cast them down and run back to the barrier. Try as he would, Glocken could not remember seeing him after that moment. Had he stood with the others before the Hulks there on the desert? Had he been slung to a huge shoulder and hauled across the waste to the cloth city and this fortress of the Apron?

"Did you . . . ?" His voice got stuck in his throat. "Where . . . that is, did you see Crustabread after . . . after the Diggers dropped us?"

Their blank faces told him even before they slowly shook their heads. Crustabread was still lying out on the desert, then, where he had fallen. They had allowed themselves to be brought away without him. But he was alive, for he had moved. Glocken clung to the thought with all his might.

Crustabread had been as alive as the rest of them when the Diggers threw them down.

But like the mud-borer that slyly slithers into the break in the wall, the doubt squirmed into his mind. Was Crusta-bread, after all these hours on the desert, alive now?

12

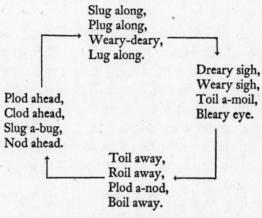

Slug along,
Plug along,
Weary-deary,
Lug along.

Dreary sigh,
Weary sigh,
Toil a-moil,
Bleary eye.

Plod ahead,
Clod ahead,
Slug a-bug,
Nod ahead.

Toil away,
Roil away,
Plod a-nod,
Boil away.

—Gummy, "Circle-rhyme," *Scribbles,*
Scroll Two (Collected Works)

Glocken was right. Crustabread *had* stirred after he was dropped by the Diggers. But once he had got his wits back into working order, he became as still as any twitch-whisker sensing danger in the air and let himself melt into a hump of invisibility under Mingy's sand-colored cloak. Inert as the desert itself, he tried to sort out what had happened and what was likely to happen next.

Even when he felt the earth shake beneath his ear, he risked no more than an eyewinker's glance. It was enough. Squeezing his eyes tighter shut, he tried to empty his mind of thought so that he wouldn't draw attention to himself.

Think like a rock or a lump of earth, his father had taught him, *and for the moment you become one.*

He heard Silky's cries and the raucous shouts of the Hulks and forced himself to flow into the very sand grains of the desert floor. Any moment now the other Minnipins would realize he wasn't with them and start searching. It wouldn't occur to them that he was deliberately hiding, for they were village folk, not of the woodland.

Sweat ran into his eyes and burned. He lay silent. One arm went numb. He didn't stir. The other arm lost its feeling, and his left leg twitched. He lay like the earth itself. He heard the departure of the Hulks, but still he hid under his cloak of invisibility. Only when he felt the return of peace to the air and to the plants about him, did he cautiously lift his head and scan the desert in all directions. Reassured, he gathered his numb arms and legs together and shakily sat and then stood up.

Behind him rose the Barrier, which they had crossed on the backs of the Diggers, and to the left, ahead, towered the mountain he had looked on all of his life—but from the other side—craggy old Frostbite. Emptiness lay in the other directions, and he wasted no time staring that way.

He was hungry and he was thirsty, and he thought with longing of the moon-melons they had left at the foot of the Barrier just a short time ago. If only he had packed a whole melon instead of the small piece that Scumble had cut for him. Perhaps when the sun set and the cool night air came, he could make the journey to the melon cache, but just now he must seek shelter from the sun's searing rays, and the nearest shelter appeared to be the face of Frostbite.

He allowed himself a careful swig of water from his flask

and then, shrugging his pack higher on his shoulders, he set off for the mountain he knew so well and yet knew not at all. He was making for the slope to the left of the dazzling white expanse that seemed fastened on the mountain like an apron. The Apron was surely the place of the Hulks, and Hulks he wanted to avoid—at least until he knew more about them.

After endless plodding under the fierce sun, he stopped to take his bearings. Squinting to shut out the glare, he tried to make out some natural pathway up the mountain ahead of him, but he was still too far away to distinguish any clear landmarks. He tried to wet his lips with his tongue, but they parched immediately.

A hundred paces more, he told himself, and then a drink. And after that, a hundred paces, two hundred paces, three hundred, four hundred. . . .

Crustabread stopped himself. He must not think about it. He must simply put one foot in front of the other until he had covered the first hundred. Seventeen . . . eighteen, nineteen . . . twenty. Just eighty more steps. And then a drink. . . . Twenty-four . . . twenty-five . . . twenty-six, build a house of thorny sticks. Thirty-one . . . thirty-two . . . thirty-three . . . thirty-four, when you go out, don't slam the door. Forty-five . . . forty-six . . . forty-seven . . . forty-eight, when the fish is caught it must be ate. Fifty . . . fifty-one, more than halfway done.

Slogging foot after slogging foot, Crustabread covered the distance. He kept himself from looking at Frostbite until he had covered the first hundred paces. The mountain seemed no nearer. He shook his flask to judge the amount of water it contained. It was perhaps half full.

A swallow now, a swallow at the end of the second hundred steps. At three hundred. . . . But his hand and throat would not obey his head's orders. When he finally tore the flask from his mouth, he dared not think how many swallows had gone down.

The punishment is two hundred paces without stopping, he ordered himself sternly.

The desert blurred before his eyes as he stumbled on. The mountain swam toward him, receded. He lost count of his steps. After a while he could not even remember why he must go forward.

A root tripped him, and he lay stretched out on the ground for he knew not how long. Here on the waste, minutes were as hours. Had he come two hundred paces? Or less? Or more? It didn't matter. He could not go on without water.

He fumbled the top off his flask and drained the last of the water. It was hot and brackish. The flask slid from his hand as he laboriously got himself on to his feet. There seemed little point in picking it up, but he forced himself to do so.

One step. Another step. And a third. One, two, three, four. Drag one foot forward, then the other. Don't stumble. Don't fall. Just keep moving.

His remaining strength was ebbing fast. The ground kept coming up to meet him, as though he were climbing some fearsome mountain. Even the plants were growing at a crazy tilt. Tilt!

Crustabread forced his heat-swollen eyelids wider open and turned slowly and carefully in his tracks.

He had reached the mountain. He was *on* the mountain. He had made it, after all.

The sun struck his head as fiercely as before, but he was no longer afraid of its power. His legs, feeble jellied stuff a moment before, stiffened into movable sticks. Shouldering his pack higher, he pushed on up the slope.

He had climbed thirty paces before he realized that the Apron had disappeared from view. Had it been a trick of the sun on the rock face? The answer was slow in coming to his gluey brain—he wondered if the heat could melt it, like butter running to the edges of a flat plate. The white Apron must be off to his right. It was hidden by a jutting spur of Frostbite—the spur that he was even now ascending.

It was his last thought of any kind for quite a while. As though they knew he was safely out of the way of any lurking Hulks, his legs dissolved under him, and he folded up between two scrawny prickle-bushes. He was vaguely surprised to find sweat still trickling down his face—surely he had dried up hours ago! In a little while the sun disappeared over the Barrier, and later it got dark. And cold. He could not remember ever having been so cold. It was freezing for a very long time before the darkness lifted. He wondered if he would ever be able to move his stiff limbs again. The light increased, until at last he felt the touch of the sun's burning hand on his shoulder. And he wondered if he would ever be cool again.

At last he moved. He started by crawling until he felt that his legs might hold him, and then with the help of a big rock he pulled himself upright and staggered on. The going became even rougher as the lower slope merged into the rock face. He had joined a sort of natural path, such as he had often found on the other side of this mountain in his own familiar valley. For a while he even thought that he was back in that valley, and then his thoughts tumbled and swirled about his head.

Occasionally his foot dislodged a stone, which went scuttering down the slope. Each time, dazed though he was, Crustabread hugged the rock face and hoped that his sandcolored cloak made him invisible to any chance watcher from below. He once tried to look down the mountain, but his head swam and heat shadows danced before his burning eyes.

The path narrowed at times to the merest foothold, and then he leeched himself to the cliff and edged sideways past the danger point. Other times he had to clamber over loose rock piles that slipped and slid treacherously beneath his feet. Now the path topped the spur and continued along a wide ledge in the direction of the other spur. Crustabread caught a glimpse off to the right of a blinding-white expanse and suddenly realized that he must be in full view of the Apron. He thrust his face into rock and thought so hard about being part of it that he could scarcely get himself unstuck from it. Cautiously, he edged forward, hugging the wall, keeping his face turned away from the Apron. His aching throat cried out for the piece of moon-melon in his pack, but there was no question of eating until he was out of sight of the Apron. He pushed himself on, step by step. The ledge was narrowing, and now the path divided. He took the upper trail.

It happened quite without warning. There was a protruding rock on which he stepped, and then suddenly the rock was no longer there. Only by slamming himself against the mountain face did he keep from going after it. The rock made a fearful racket as it bounced down the steep slope, dislodging other rocks, which clattered after it, and then, from far below, came a sound that he wasn't expecting—a splash.

A splash. The meaning of it seeped slowly into his sluggish brain. A splash . . . water. . . . But he had known all along in the dim recesses of his mind, surely. . . . Known and not known. Known that when he found a pond backing up from a stream, he would find a Slaptail's dam across that stream. Known that the flooding of the Watercress must be caused by a dam. Known from the moment he saw the white Apron joining the natural spurs of Frostbite that it must be a dam—not built by Slaptails, but by beings far greater than any seen before by Minnipin.

He could feel his hands slipping on the rock face. Cautiously he felt with first his left foot and then his right for a crevice or an outcropping to save himself from sliding down into the deep waters of the dam.

There was nothing.

Crazily he wondered what sort of advice Muggles' *Maxims* would give at this moment. And he thought about the four Water Gapians being carried off by the Hulks.

Now there was suddenly less than nothing for his feet to cling to, for they were dangling in space. Powerless to help himself, he clutched vainly at the cliff while his body slowly, slowly slid out and down.

This was the end of him then. He had never got his piece of moon-melon, he thought regretfully. He might as well have eaten it there on the desert floor when his thirst was so great.

This was the way his father and mother had gone. And now he, too—the last, the very last of his family. There would never be another Crustabread, ever.

He could no longer feel the pressure of rock on his chest and realized that most of him was hanging in space. He pressed his face tight against the cliff and clung with the

remaining strength of his numbed fingers. Slowly, inexorably, inevitably, he slid down, until only his hands clung to the lip of the shelf. He felt a terrible regret for all the life he would never see or feel or taste, and then his fingers grasped only space, and he was falling.

He hit something with a terrible jolt, and he had time to think of the way a rock bounced down a hill. Then there was a curious sound in his ears, like a whisper. Like the whisper of a tree harp when the soft sunny wind plays through it. Or the inner sound of cloud puffs in a blue summer sky. Or the deep still music of sun slanting into the birch woods.

So this is dying, Crustabread thought. Dying is a whisper of music. And then, as far as he knew, he died.

13

Once upon a whisper-time—so it is said, but who would believe it?—when the Minnipins were seeking a new dwelling-place during the Dry Time, they arose one morning to find their water gone from their casks, and they wept, but no tears came for they were so dry; upon which the Glocken of Then played upon his bells and brought water forth gushing at their feet—enough to fill their casks to overflowing. But the water tasted of skink-root, and the bells could do nothing about that, and *this* I believe.

—Pretend-story told by Glocken
to Glocken to Glocken, from
Then to Now

Not being able to talk did something odd to time—made it stretch out longer. When Glocken demanded if any of them had seen Crustabread, Scumble was able to examine everybody's face three times over before anybody spoke. It was like watching Minnipin children play *Fleeing the Mushrooms* when one of them forgot what he was supposed to say. Even the oddly-fitting white garments were like costumes. . . .

Then everybody talked at once, until Gam Lutie clapped her hands together.

"We must tell the Red-Carrot-one at once," she said. "He can send the Stickermen to find Crustabread."

"No," said Silky. "Give him a chance to get away."

"Get away where?" asked Glocken. "By this time the Diggers have gone back over the Barrier. He will perish on the sand."

"The Hulks seem friendly enough," Gam Lutie said. "And the swords gave no warning against them."

"How do you know what the swords are doing?" demanded Silky. "The Carrot still has them."

"Nonsense," said Gam Lutie briskly. "If we ask for them, of course he will give them back to us."

"He gave me the Whisper Stone," Glocken said slowly. "Though he didn't much want to. But he kept the *Maxims*. He said he would pay Muggles a good price. *And* the gold he kept." Glocken frowned thoughtfully. "He didn't offer to pay for that."

"In any case," said Gam Lutie in her crispest tones, "we have no choice. Crustabread is on the desert, and he will surely die there. These Hulks, though they are uncouth and ugly beyond appetite, seem friendly. They are interested in us and our welfare. The Red Carrot told me so himself. I shall go and tell him about Crustabread." She walked determinedly to the door and pushed on it.

But it was fastened against her. Unbelieving, she pushed harder and then, her lips primmed together, pounded on it with her fists. A voice shouted something from outside so loudly that they could not distinguish the words, but Gam Lutie stopped pounding and waited. There was a rattle and a grating sound as of a drawn bolt; then the door opened, and a great inquiring eye looked through the crack.

"I demand to know," said Gam Lutie, "by what right you lock us in here. Take me to your leader at once."

"Unh, yes," the voice came in a grumble, like trees falling. The door opened wider, and now they saw the rest of the Stickerman. Under his hat, which said he was Number Thirty, huge pale eyes looked out of a thick bumpy face, and his lower lip hung loose. His hair sprouts were blue-black, as was what hair they could see under his hat. Scumble gave a silent shudder, but Gam Lutie marched through the door with her usual certainty. The door swung shut after her with a bang and a rattle and a clang of metal.

"That was the ugliest Hulk of all," said Glocken into the startled silence.

Whistling through his teeth, Scumble walked over and gave a push at the big panel. It remained obstinately shut. He was sure that it would.

"Gam Lutie shouldn't tell them about Crustabread," Silky declared. "If he had wanted to come inside with us, he would have come forward. Don't you see? He stayed in the desert purposely so he could get us out of here."

Glocken looked glum. "He'll never do it. How can one Minnipin fight against Hulks like these?"

Silky's eyes raked him with scorn. "You're the one who's always full of tales of heroes. How do you think *they* got started? By sitting down and giving up the moment things look bad? Why don't you do something?"

"But I . . ." He looked helplessly round the room. "There's only the door, and it's bolted. And that window up there—it's much too high to reach and has bars on it besides. It's hopeless. I'm not a Digger who can climb up a wall."

"No, I suppose not. I'm sorry, Glocken." Silky turned

slowly away. "Do you think," she asked in a low voice, "do you think the Wafer is all right?"

"How could I know!" Glocken said crossly. "If you want to worry, you had better worry about *us*— Oh, of course he's all right, Silky. We would have *seen* him if he hadn't gone off with the Diggers."

"I don't know," said Silky, still turned away. "We didn't *look* for him, and you know how the Diggers blend into the color of the ground. . . ." She clasped her hands and brought them tremblingly to her lips.

Scumble wished he had words to comfort her, but he wouldn't be able to say them even if they came into his mind, so he looked round for something to do—anything that would be a busy-ness. There was the high, barred window, and though he could think of no way of getting rid of the bars, at least he might be able to look out, and it would be some sort of action.

The rough-hewn table and four rock slabs didn't seem enough to build a stairway to the high window, but it was a start. So Scumble started.

He took hold of the huge table and pulled on it with all his might. It gave a shiver and a shudder and moved, perhaps half-an-ear's length. Another tug and the table groaned. With a little shriek it gave up a whole ear's length.

"Must you make that noise? What *are* you doing?" demanded Silky.

What you said, Scumble answered within himself. *I'm doing something*. He pointed to the window and then shielded his eyes with his hand as though looking into the distance.

"You'll never reach the window even standing on the table," said Glocken impatiently. "The table's not high enough."

Scumble shrugged and went on pushing. *I'll think of something else then,* he thought. *When I get halfway up.*

"Well," said Silky suddenly, "at least he's *trying.* Let's help."

With paralyzing slowness they moved the high table over beneath the window. Amongst the three of them they managed to get the smallest of the stones up on the table. But that was the end of it. They could not raise the other three off the floor.

"Now what?" asked Glocken.

Scumble rubbed his hands on his coarse white cloak and took hold of a table leg. Laboriously he pulled himself up until he was standing on the table and stepped on the stone slab. By stretching mightily he could just touch the window ledge with the tips of his fingers.

Silky clapped her hands together. "If you could just see outside! Glocken, quick! Climb up and let Scumble stand on your back."

Grumblingly, Glocken complied. When he had got himself settled tailor-fashion on the slab, Scumble mounted to his shoulders.

"What do you see?" demanded Silky, dancing up and down.

Scumble shook his head. Gripping the iron bars, he pulled himself up to get a better view.

"What do you *see?*" Silky insisted, while Glocken gave a grunt and wiggled his shoulders. "Oh, *can't* you talk!?"

He was looking down, and what he saw would have

robbed him of speech if the Essence of Emptie had not already done so. The tower looked out upon a tremendous basin of water, glinting gold in the westering sun. Beneath his window was a ledge of washed limestone, and by craning his neck, he was able to follow it with his eye. At either end of the Apron-dam, it joined the natural rock of the mountain spurs.

"Come on down," ordered Glocken. "My shoulders are sinking."

But Scumble paid no attention. Had that been a movement on the mountain just across the water? He squinched his eyes to see better.

"Somebody's coming. Quick!" cried Silky.

The very room seemed to shake with the noise of approaching footsteps.

Wait a minute, Scumble tried to cry, straining desperately to see better.

"Get down. Get DOWN!" cried Silky. "They're coming."

Glocken was wriggling so that it was impossible to stay at the window. Yet he must try, somehow, to. . . . In desperate haste Scumble worked at the coarse knot of his cloak-collar with one hand while he clutched the window bar with his other. His fingers shook, but he somehow got the knot undone, and the collar transferred from his neck to the bar.

"Scumble, the sun has boiled your brain!" cried Silky.

He tied a new knot—with teeth and fingers—and with the last of his strength he stuffed the cloak out of the window.

"Down!" Glocken grabbed his ankles.

An instant before Glocken yanked at him, Scumble saw something that made him grip the iron bars with both hands.

It was directly below the spot where he had seen the movement. A great slab burst away from the mountain and went chunking down into the water. He heard the splash, but he didn't see it, for he was straining his eyes for signs of the figure he thought he had seen toiling along the face of the mountain—if it really was a figure.

Yes, there it was—sprawled now against the new scar on the rock face. But—

As Glocken yanked at his ankles again, Scumble saw the sprawling figure slip down the scarred rock face. It bounced. And then—it was as though Scumble felt the jar. Not that instant, but a moment later. He sensed that he was falling, but he couldn't be falling, for he was still gripping the iron bar in his hand. There was a singing in his head as though he had been standing in Glocken's bell tower during the playing of the carillon. Then he landed on the table with a squunk and bounced from there to the floor in a heap.

He was aware of the door opening and Gam Lutie coming in, but though her voice and Silky's registered, they seemed to come from a distance. The strange, wonderful ringing was still in his ears.

"Very civil, the Red Carrot," Gam Lutie was saying. "I don't believe we need worry about our safety in the slightest."

"What's so civil about locking us in a prison?" demanded Silky.

"He explained all that," said Gam Lutie. "It is for our own protection. Many of the workers are rude fellows like those who attacked us in the square. What *is* that hullabaloo!"

The shouting and running had started below almost immediately after Scumble's fall. It was part and parcel of the whole weird happening. But now the shouts were coming nearer—up the steps. Suddenly the door burst open, and two enormous Hulks pounded in, thrusting aside Silky and Gam Lutie. They narrowly missed Scumble, still hunched on the floor, their eyes intent on the wall, on which a long crack had appeared.

Scumble looked stupidly from the crack to the iron bar which he still held in his hand. How had he done *that?*

The Hulks exclaimed loudly and then turned and slammed out of the room, still paying no attention to the prisoners. Somewhere a wailing whistle started up, like a warning.

Silky was the first to regain her voice. "They didn't bolt the door!" Triumphantly she crossed the floor and pushed against it. It swung open a little way. "We can leave!"

Gam Lutie shook her head. "The Red Carrot said we would be safe here. Really, we must not go against the order of things."

"What did he say about Crustabread?"

Gam Lutie looked abashed. "I . . . that is, I didn't . . . we didn't . . . well, to be quite honest, I hadn't got that far when we were interrupted. Two Stickermen came running in, shouting something, and the Red Carrot ran out, and one of the Hulks brought me up here."

Silky stared at her for a long moment. Then she pushed the door open wider. "I'm going out," she announced. "The rest of you can come or not, depending on what you're made of—bone and blood or puffer-dough."

Scumble laboriously got to his feet to follow. Gam Lutie hesitated and then fell into line.

"Coming, Glocken?" asked Silky.

Scumble realized that Glocken hadn't stirred. He was still crouched on the table, but it might be said that he wasn't there at all. It was as though he was listening to something so far away and so long ago that he had gone halfway to meet it.

"Glocken!" Gam Lutie said sharply.

He dropped his eyes to look at them and through them.

"Glocken!" Silky's voice was suddenly frightened. "Glocken, come down!"

He blinked as though seeing her for the first time. "Did you . . ." His voice was changed, wondering. . . . "Didn't you hear it?"

"How could I help but hear it! They make enough noise with their clumping feet!"

Glocken brushed away the subject of Hulks with a wave of his hand. "Not that. It was just before Scumble came down." He appealed to Scumble. "Did you hear it?"

Scumble felt the skin crawl on the back of his neck. He suddenly knew what Glocken meant—the strange, sweet ringing, like . . . like . . .

Glocken nodded. "You *did* hear it. Don't you see? Don't you understand? It was the Whisper. The Whisper of Glocken."

14

If he's as wise as he is small,
The Mouse
Won't let the hooter-bird construct
His house.

—Gummy, *Scribbles*, Scroll Two
(Collected Works)

Once beyond the door of their tower room and at the head of the great echoing stone stairs, Scumble suddenly wished he could turn back to the safety of their prison. But the others didn't falter, and Scumble was ashamed to show his own terrible fears.

The shouts and slammings had dwindled to only an occasional banging about, and by the time they had toiled down the big steps to the next level, the only sound that bounced off the chill walls was the pat of their soft slippers. Scumble felt a new pulse-beat of alarm in his throat. Was the crack so bad, then, that the Hulks had deserted the tower entirely—forgetting their captives in their rush to save themselves? A crack in a dam was the same whether it was Minnipin-high or Hulk-high. Powerful as the Hulks appeared, the power of the Watercress River was far greater.

They came to a landing halfway down the next flight, and an open doorway that gave onto a platform or balcony. Scumble plucked at Silky's cloak and pointed to it. She hesitated, then gave a quick nod, and they all filed out onto the platform, blinking in the sudden shower of light.

The sterile desert spread before them, vaster than anything they had ever imagined. Only the looming Barrier on the right broke the monotony of flat plain, and it had a monotony of its own, for it marched along the desert as far as the eye could see. The cloth city at the base of the white Apron, with its hurrying figures and its din of activity, shrank into insignificance.

"I'm frightened," said Silky in a still, small voice. "I'm thinking that perhaps I don't want to go out there after all."

Scumble took her hand and patted it reassuringly, but rather absently. He might never have another chance to view a damsite from such a vantage point, and he was determined to make the best of this one. What he saw from this platform made his own sluice-gate operations look like children's water-play. Directly below them, it was plain to see from here, was the old water-course of the river—a watercourse which was filled in now with earth and level with the surrounding plain, but showing as a darker gray-brown streak winding through the gray-brown desert. The river must have flowed through a canyon, wasting itself on sterile rock instead of feeding the land. Scumble drew in his breath in admiration for the enormous scheme that the Hulks had carried out.

"I see green," Gam Lutie said suddenly. "Over there."

They followed her pointing finger to the left, beyond the spur, and Scumble nodded. Yes, it would be green over there. The Hulks had turned the Watercress somehow so that they could build their dam. And when the dam was finished, they had blocked off the diversion to allow the river to flow again on its usual way through the mountain, ending inside the walls of the dam. From here it would be let out a little at a time as it was needed to make the desert green. There must be giant sluice-gates below, controlled by powerful machinery—nothing like his own contrivance in Water Gap. . . .

"Let's get on down," said Silky, "while there's nobody around."

They met no one, heard nothing but far-off shouting, as they traveled down the steps, passing one landing and then another and another. Doors swung carelessly on their hinges, chairs were tipped over as though Hulks had got up in a hurry.

Scumble rubbed his running-wet face with his sleeve when they finally reached the ground floor and walked into the sunlit room where the Red Carrot had sat. It, too, was deserted. Scumble plucked at Glocken's sleeve and pointed to a door opposite them. Glocken only looked dazed, so Scumble pulled at Silky and Gam Lutie and made gestures to indicate that they should take a hasty departure. Silky nodded and started for the door, the rest trailing after.

At the last minute Scumble turned aside. The four Minnipin swords were still lying cold and inert on the table. They remained inert and cold and heavy when Scumble had parceled them out to the others and they had buckled them on. Was it possible that the magic had gone out of the swords?

When they swung back the great door, a blast of heat and noise struck them full force. For a moment they could see nothing in the blaze of sunlight but white shapes billowing and skimming past. . . . Gradually the white shapes turned into hurrying Hulks. They were carrying all manner of bundles and were headed in one direction—the loading platform. Some were pushing carts loaded high with packs and bundles. Most of the flapping houses that had faced the Apron had now been struck.

Scumble touched Silky, pointed in the direction of the loading platform and the spur beyond; but she looked frightened and drew back. Impatiently Scumble took her arm and drew her after him. There seemed no way to explain that there was danger of the dam bursting and that they were standing at the most dangerous place. So he simply dragged her along protesting, and the others followed because there was nothing else to do.

Scumble was thinking furiously. There was no use trying to find Crustabread. He was mortally sure that he had seen Crustabread plunge to his death inside the dam. Their first concern then was to get to a place of safety, and that seemed to be the spur. The activity increased as they got closer to the loading platform. Oddly, no one tried to stop them or even so much as to shout at them. Perhaps the white clothing they wore acted as a sort of disguise, or perhaps the Hulks simply valued their lives above their curiosity. Scumble turned his full attention to the loading platform while he had the chance. What if he could build something like that in Water Gap connecting the high bank with the sarcen field on the low bank. The time and work it would save! And on holidays folk could ride it for pleasure. Who knows what would develop next! Perhaps one day there could be whining-cords stretching all the way to Deep-as-a-Well, to Slipper-on-the-Water, to—to Watersplash at the head of the valley!

"Look in there," said Gam Lutie in an awed voice. On their right they had come abreast of a huge doorway opening into a shallow high-ceilinged chamber running along the wall of the dam. The hall was but dimly lit and cluttered with vague shapes.

"CLEAR THE WAY! CLEAR THE WAY!" bawled a voice. There were more shouts and then a thundering that shook the earth beneath their feet.

Bearing down upon them from behind was a gigantic piece of machinery on wheels. It was led by a crew of the great Hulks, who cleared a path by shouting at everyone in their way.

"CLEAR THE WAY! MOVE!" they bawled at the Minnipins.

There was only one direction to go, and that was through the huge doorway. They whisked inside and scuttered under a big wooden framework on blocks that was standing against the wall, just by the opening. There were voices and hammerings from other parts of the vast, barny building, but nobody was close at hand.

For a while they simply huddled under the framework; then Scumble got curious and stuck his head out to see what went on in this place. It must be a workshop. He could make out shapes of carts, some of them without their wheels, and machines that had no meaning for him and machines that had. There was a pulley and a gear-wheel contraption. . . . Satisfied, he twisted his neck round still further to look up at the framework they were sheltering under. Roof, windows. . . . Why, it was a sort of house!

"Ssst," warned Silky, and Scumble ducked back under the framework just in time. A pair of tree-trunks clumped past and came to stop in the big doorway. In a moment it was joined by another pair. Down at one end of the workshop a hammer began to clang. But Scumble had become interested in this house they were scrooched under. Though it was up on blocks now, it was clearly made to be put on wheels. And at the end away from the doorway were steps dangling down to the floor. It was a good-sized house—for a Minnipin. Scumble wondered how Hulks could ever fit into it. But the idea appealed to him—a house on wheels that could be rolled from place to place. Quarrel with your neighbor Klop the Cobbler and move your house next to Carver the Toy-maker. . . .

He suddenly shivered. How would you ever know you had reached home if your house could roll away while you were gone?

"More tree-trunks going past," came the warning, this time from Gam Lutie.

And then there was a "Ssst" from the shadowy end of the framework. Silky had found the dangling steps and was climbing them.

Two pairs of the tree-trunks stopped beside Scumble, their voices booming out like Prize the Baker's gong that he struck when he had pulled a batch of sugar-tailed mice out of the oven, Scumble withdrew and silently followed Gam Lutie and Glocken, who were going up the dangling steps after Silky. The first step was high off the ground, but after that they were comfortable Minnipin-size treads. They walked through a door-shaped opening into—

It really *was* a house! A house with four chairs and a table. A house with cozy-looking beds built right into the wall. Cupboards. Chests of drawers. The work was crude, with big chisel marks, but after their struggles with Hulk-sized furniture, this room looked almost like home.

And then Silky poked at him and pointed at the windows. They were barred.

Outside a great voice bawled, "DANGER'S OVER!"

Silence met this announcement, to be followed at once by a great stir and a roar of voices. Of a sudden, the house gave a jolt and all four Minnipins were thrown to the floor.

Had the dam burst, after all? Picking himself up and dazedly helping the others, Scumble heard the laughter of the Hulks outside.

"Almost knocked the cage right over!"

"You break up the midgelings' house, and there'll be something to answer for."

Cage! Midgelings' house? For a moment the words carried no meaning. Scumble's forehead scrooged up to help his brain work, and then he caught sight of Silky's wide eyes and dropped mouth, and he somehow read there the meaning of the Hulk's words.

It was for *them*. The house was for *them!* Minnipins! Gam Lutie and Silky and Glocken and himself. And it was a cage because there were iron bars at the windows. They were to be caged like woodmice that Minnipin children sometimes kept as pets!

"Midgelings!" Gam Lutie was aghast.

"A cage . . ." whispered Silky. "Oh I couldn't stand that. We must get away from this terrible place. Glocken. . . ."

For the first time since he had heard the Whisper sound, Glocken came out of his daze long enough to nod in agreement. "Though you understand I must find it . . ." he murmured, and went right back inside himself.

Scumble straightened his shoulders. It appeared that if anybody was going to get them away, he would have to do the doing. Get away—but where? Crustabread would have known. Crustabread. . . . Scumble's mouth fell open.

But that must be what Crustabread was about when he fell to his death! He was finding a way across Frostbite. Surely it was so. And if Crustabread had looked to Frostbite as the only way out, then Frostbite must be the way. They would try for Frostbite!

The Hulks finally stopped leaning against the cage-house and went off about their work, and the doorway to the outside stood empty. The New Heroes scrambled down the steps and darted along the wall to the opening.

Scumble's heart sank. When he and the others first made their escape from the tower, the Hulks were too intent on clearing their goods and themselves from the path of the pent-up water to pay much attention to four beings half their size, also fleeing for their lives. But now that the danger was past, the Hulks were moving more casually, calling back and forth to each other, taking relief in boisterous laughter.

The New Heroes got through the big door, but they had scarcely come abreast of the loading platform when they were spotted.

"HEIGH! Look here!"

"It's the MINNOWS!"

"The FREAKS!"

Within the instant the Minnipins were surrounded by the great rank-smelling beings, who squatted down to inspect them better.

"I like the one with the SILKY HAIR. . . ."

"This one looks like a BITER. Watch your FINGERS!"

"Heigh, THIS minnow's a queer one. He's got a MAD LIGHT in his eyes."

"And THAT little duffer there! He's going to run me through with his PEN-KNIFE!"

A howl of laughter went up that beat against Scumble's ears. And the noise, the confusion, his anger and frustration so crowded in upon him that he could only see a red haze.

Surely the sword of the Minnipins could not fail him now. Inert and heavy it felt in his hand. But he lifted it and brought it down as hard as he could on his tormentor's hand.

The sword only bounced.

The shout of jeering laughter that went up then brought prickles of tears to Scumble's eyes.

But now a new sound was heard. It was the same whistle that had dispersed the crowd before, when the Minnipins had been brought to the dam. The flashing silver helmets appeared, and the billy-clubs laid about, until all the Hulks had slunk off to their work and the special guards had scooped up the Minnipins and bore them back. Back to the tower.

The Red Carrot was in his chair behind the table. He spoke kindly to them, though Scumble felt his kindness was carefully laid over irritation.

"I am sorry that my people have alarmed you. But really, you brought it on yourselves by going out without any guards."

"We were frightened," said Gam Lutie, every word dripping its own icicle. "So much running and shouting. And then everybody disappeared."

186

"We wanted to know what was going on," Silky put in.

"Ah, yes," said the Red Carrot. "Our warning-system showed a slight tremor, but fortunately it was not great enough to do any damage to the dam. I'm sorry you were frightened."

"We want to go home," Gam Lutie said bluntly.

The Carrot leaned back in his chair. "Ah yes . . . of course. And we are going to see that you get home. But . . . ah . . ." and he leaned forward so that they could inspect the pores in his face. "I am certain that my people will want to help your people, since it is our dam which has destroyed your valley. There is no doubt that we will send help to your valley. We will see that everybody is moved out to a new home, which we will construct for you, in payment for the damage we have caused."

His great pink tongue came out and traveled once around his lips. "But first . . ."

Scumble could see that Gam Lutie was drawing herself up.

"We do not wish," she pronounced, "to be moved out of our valley."

The Carrot looked perplexed. "But don't you see that it will be impossible to live there any longer? I thought you understood. The dam—"

"Remove your dam," said Gam Lutie.

The Carrot stared at her for a time. "I see," he said at last. He joined his fingers together so that they looked like a tumble of bleached cucumbers and studied them. "Let me make you a proposition," he said after some more time had crept by. "Since my people have never seen anyone like you, it may be difficult to convince them that we should remove our dam so that you can go on living in your valley. You understand that I, myself, am powerless to act without their sanction. Now it has just occurred to me that there is a very simple way to overcome their opposition and at the same time benefit your people in other ways. I propose that we arrange for you to meet my people. What do you think of that?"

"Just what do you mean?" asked Gam Lutie.

The Red Carrot looked from one to the other thoughtfully. "What do you say to visiting my country? Come, you have a spirit of adventure, or you wouldn't have traveled so far to see what was happening to your river. We could show you all of our land, and perhaps you, too, could help us by telling us of your lives. . . ."

Gam Lutie's eyes were beginning to spark fiercely, and Scumble trembled lest she give away their knowledge of the cage-house. It seemed important to keep what they knew to themselves.

It was Glocken, wandering out of his reverie for a moment, who forged the crafty question. "And how are we to travel?" he asked. "Are we to be carried like children once more?"

The fat pink tongue came out and made another trip around the thick lips. "Not at all," the Carrot assured them. "I shall see that you aren't touched again. Why"—he hesitated and then, as though the idea had just come to him—"I'll have my men build a special carriage for you. It will be . . . well, what would you say to a little house that you can actually live in? A house on wheels! I believe it could be done." He sat back in his chair and looked from one to another, smiling and smiling.

But Scumble knew, and the others knew that the smile was only a front for skullduggery. It was a teaspoonful of honey coating a bitter gallroot. The house the Red Carrot spoke of was already built and ready to go on its wheels. It had bars on its windows, and no doubt when the door was put on, it would have a stout lock.

Whether they consented or not made no difference. They were prisoners of the Hulks, and if they were ever to see the Land Between the Mountains again, it would take a greater magic than they now possessed.

15

A puff of dust
On a desert rise;

A sun-warmed scent,
Whimpering cries;
And trusting, deep,
Two greeny eyes;

Stringy arms,
An almost-nose;
Needle-sharp
Fingers, toes;

And deep inside,
A heart that glows.

—Gummy, *Scribbles*, Scroll Two
(Collected Works)

When Crustabread's thoughts filtered back into his head, the very first one was a sort of left-over memory—the memory of a sweet whisper. He had taken it for the whisper of death, but now he wasn't so sure. By all odds he should be at the bottom of the dam, but if that were true, he had learned to breathe like a trout. Odd—it didn't seem to matter very much, now that it had happened, whatever it was that *had* happened. At least he was out of the sun's glare. He would just rest here while he waited for the next thing to happen. No hurry about opening his eyes to see where he was. If he was dead, he wouldn't be able to open them anyway; and if he was alive, he didn't feel up to facing whatever had to be faced just now.

After a while it occurred to him that he had no business being dead. You couldn't just selfishly go off dead, leaving your friends to their fate, and still feel easy in your mind.

With a deep sigh he opened his eyes. But it took a little time to understand what he was looking at. There was sunscorched sky out there, but it was cut off from him by—by — Didn't that sheered-off stone face directly overhead look somehow familiar? Swiveling his neck set up an agonizing pain behind his eyes, but he got the impression of protective walls on either side—like a cave with no roof . . . a cave with no roof . . . a cave with no roof. . . .

His thoughts went out of his head once more, leaving swirling blackness, but when they trickled back again, they were stronger. . . . A cave with no roof . . . a cave with no roof. . . . Why did he keep saying that—like the refrain of a song? He squinted up at the sky, past the somehow-familiar scar on the mountain above the opening of his cave . . . his cave. . . . That was it! He was in a cave with no roof. And the scar was where the protruding rock had been —the rock that had given way under his foot. It was all coming back to him. He had clung with his very fingernails to the sheer rock face but had felt himself slipping, slipping. Then at last had come the moment when his fingers touched space instead of wall, and he thought that was the end of him. But he had only fallen to the outthrust lip of this cave.

He wasn't at all dead then! He couldn't even be very badly injured, for he had fallen only from the top of the cave. Just a thump on the head, probably, a head already weakened after the long ordeal on the desert. He had only been knocked a bit foolish.

Encouraged, he slowly sat up, hands upheld to catch his foolish head if it should roll off. Food was the first thing. Food would make his legs strong again. As he struggled and strained to get the pack off his shoulders, he thought of the moon-melon—of the cool, watery chunks laving his parched throat. His fingers shook with excitement as he fumbled the pack open . . . and stared blankly at the terrible shambles inside. Smashed clay jars leaked nut oil into the glutinous remains of watercress jell and salted currant seeds. And mixed in with the splintered clay, the oil, the sweet, and the salt, mingling the flavors into a vast unsavory stew, was the overlying mush of the moon-melon. Crustabread's mind was still so woolly that he found it hard to think. Slowly it came to him that he must have landed full on the pack when he fell.

He found that it was possible to eat the dreadful mess if he closed his eyes, held his nose, and separated the food from the splinters by feel. He swallowed every bit of food that he could ferret out of the pack, though it was little enough. Once the unsavory meal was finished, he felt a bit better and even able to think of the next step. For a start, he inched farther out on the ledge in front of his cave and peeped over, only to pull himself back with a mighty jerk. He was at a giddy height over a vast bowl of water.

It was no wonder the Minnipin valley was flooded past Deep-as-a-Well!

And if the height of the dazzling white dam across from him was any indication, the Land Between the Mountains would be flooded all the way from Frostbite to Snowdrift before the Hulks were finished. The sun was slipping behind the Barrier, and Crustabread was able to look at the dam without squinting. A slaptail couldn't have chosen a better place. Two long spurs jutted out from Frostbite, one on each side of him, and the dam joined them to make the fourth side of the bowl. It was a monstrously thick dam, tapering to a wide flat top. In the very center, directly across from him, a tower reared above the dam wall. It had a small, barred window. Crustabread started to draw back into greater invisibility when a movement caught his eye. It was only a billowing cloth hanging stark white from the window, but, strangely, it had the shape of a Minnipin out walking in a high wind.

Crustabread chewed his lip.

The next instant he jerked his head with a start that set it pounding again, for his quick ears had caught a curious sound—a tiny sound that hadn't been there before. A scrabbling, dragging sort of sound as though someone was making his quiet way along the face of the mountain. Just above him. An unknown step. Not a Minnipin, for his friends could not move so quietly. Nor a Hulk.

Cautiously he twisted his head until the pain stopped him. It was enough. He was looking straight up—into the greeny eyes of a familiar wizened face.

It was the Wafer.

He made little chittering sounds and suddenly plummeted directly into Crustabread's arms, all but hurling both of them over the edge.

"Let me look at you," said Crustabread, hauling him back to safety. The wrappings on the Wafer's hurt leg were shredded and his wound worn raw. He looked as though he hadn't eaten or slept since they left the Barrier. Crustabread touched the small head wonderingly.

"Better you had followed the trail of your own folk," he said. "This looks like being a full stop."

The greeny eyes watched him without wavering.

"Let's see what I can do." Crustabread set the Wafer down and rummaged again in his knapsack. There was precious little left besides splinters, but he scraped at the cloth with a spoon until he had something to offer. The little Digger made faces but obediently swallowed the offering, then began to make clicking sounds, which seemed to be the nearest he could come to speech, and pointed upward.

"No thank you," said Crustabread. "That's a one-way rock for me. I think I'm going to try to go over there," and he pointed to the billowing cloth that beckoned from across the dam.

The Wafer's gray-brown face seemed to turn grayer, and he clicked and chittered louder and faster. He pointed his needle-finger at the dam and shook his head violently.

"Yes, I know," said Crustabread, "but I've got to try to get the others out. I've got to get Gam Lutie and Silky and —" He stopped short at the sudden eager light in the Wafer's eyes. "Yes, Silky," he repeated. "I believe that Silky is over there," and he pointed at the tower.

It was dangerous, and he had no way of knowing for sure that the Minnipins were enclosed in the tower. And if they were, and he could get them out, what good would that do? Possibly they would all perish on the mountain. Perhaps the Hulks actually meant no harm. . . . Crustabread let his eyes drop from the tower to the swollen mass of water collected behind the dam. Whether they meant harm or not, he thought, they had caused it.

It wouldn't be long before dark. Until then, he would seek out with his eyes the path he would take from the cave round to the top of the dam wall, and so along to the window of the tower. After that, he would have to see.

He settled himself with his back against the fallen rubble and smoothed a place beside him for the Wafer. But the baby Digger ignored the spot and planted himself on Crustabread's lap, his head cradled on Crustabread's chest.

Crustabread put his arm protectively around the little creature. It seemed a long time since he had comforted a wild thing, and the very act suddenly gave him hope.

The night caught him by surprise again, coming down like a cloak thrown over his head. Crustabread waited no longer than it took for his eyes to accustom themselves to the darkness. Then, lifting the Wafer to his shoulder, he started out on the path that would lead him to the cloak that flapped like a Minnipin in a high wind.

16

History is based on Facts: niggling-small Facts, pothering-medium Facts, whopping-large Facts. And the greatest of all these is the Fact of Magic.

—Walter the Earl, *Glorious True Facts in the History of the Min- nipins from the Beginning to the Year of Gammage 880.*

The Stickerman who took the four Minnipins up the echoing stone staircase the second time was the one with the thick bumpy face and the pale eyes. Number Thirty.

Number Thirty was in no mood to pretend that he was escorting guests. From the very beginning he treated the Minnipins for what they were—his prisoners.

He herded them up the stairs, but when Scumble and Silky, who were in the lead, stopped on the fourth step for a breather, he gave an exasperated sigh that almost blew them down. Then he bellowed for another Stickerman to help him, and Scumble thought his earholes must collapse. Of a sudden, his feet went out from under him, and the next moment he was being jounced and bounced up the stairs, his head barely missing each step. He was pinioned under Number Thirty's left arm like a sack of second-grade sarcen, with head and feet dangling. He caught sight of Silky swinging in like manner on the other side, and Gam Lutie's indignant cries mounted the stairs behind him.

Scumble had a terrible and unaccountable desire to laugh, and as his head swung toward each new step, only to be withdrawn at the last instant before his skull cracked on the edge, his stomach choked and writhed with the effort of keeping his laughter from bursting forth in great guffaws. He was becoming light-headed, he tried to tell himself soberly, but the chuckling feeling rose again to his chest, and he bit his lips to keep it from rolling out.

They were all dumped unceremoniously on the floor of the tower chamber, gloomy now with the fast falling of night, the barred window high above them a square of blue-gray. Flickering lantern light from the landing cut a shape on the floor through the open door. A third Stickerman brought a tray of smoking hot food and placed it on the floor before them. He and the second Stickerman departed quickly, but Number Thirty looked down at the four dejected Heroes with gloating eyes.

"We must have more light," Gam Lutie said briskly, and on the instant Scumble felt the laughter inside him turn to sobs.

"*Must* you now!" snarled Number Thirty. He wheeled and strode through the door, slamming and bolting it behind him. He gave a final roar through the crack. "Don't try any of your tricks on me! If it wasn't for you, I would be riding the carts back to my own country right now instead of nursing four midgelings."

Scumble hauled himself up on his elbows and examined the tray of food as best he could in the darkness. It smelled strongly of onions and herbs, and he was suddenly realizing that he had eaten nothing since the day before when the Stickermen had brought them in from the desert. Gingerly, he poked an exploratory finger into the dark gravy that covered a lumpy something and tasted. He was just reaching the finger out for more when, without any warning, his throat caught fire. Choking, sputtering, gasping, he caught up one of the four cups and took a swallow. A moment later he was spewing out the bitter stuff. Tears sprang to his eyes.

"What is it?" Gam Lutie asked in alarm.

"It's not—it's not *poisoned*, is it?" Silky asked.

Glocken put out his hand wonderingly and dipped into a white mound on a plate.

No, don't! Scumble, still strangling from the assault of hot spices on his mouth and throat, tried to stop him. *No, don't!* And "No," he at last croaked out of his stiff voice box so long unused, "DON'T!"

Glocken left his mouth hanging open, his finger suspended in air. Gam Lutie's hand flew to her throat.

"You said something!" cried Silky. "You can talk again!"

"I—I—" Scumble gulped out, but that was the best he could do. His voice failed him again.

"It's all right," said Gam Lutie. "Your voice will come again. But don't strain . . ."

"Sh-h-h," said Glocken suddenly, "listen."

"Is it the Whisper?" breathed Silky. "Do you hear the Whisper again?"

Glocken shook his head, pointed toward the door.

Number Thirty had apparently settled himself against the door of their prison lest they somehow try to sneak past him. His snarls had gradually worn away to grunts and finally sank to heavy breathing—for all the world like the sound of Goldfoil the Smith's bellows. Occasionally the bellows made room for a rude belch, or they ran out of air, but each time they picked up again with a blast and a shudder and settled down to a regular rhythm once more.

"He's surely asleep," said Gam Lutie after a while.

Glocken gave a nod.

"Then shouldn't we be doing something?" Silky jumped up, but her foot caught on the tray, and there was a great crash and rattle of crockery. She caught her breath.

The bellows sighed like the north wind through the trees and then took up their old refrain.

"Yes, we should," said Gam Lutie as though there had been no interruption. She stood up and gave herself a brisk shake. "I entirely agree. I have no wish to be kept in a cage and displayed like a turtle with two heads. Furthermore, we should all starve to death if we had to eat the Hulks' food for very long."

Scumble scaled the table first and then gave a hand to Glocken. Number Thirty had not bothered to remove the rock slab that they had labored so hard to put there hours before, so Glocken had only to anchor himself on it and brace himself for Scumble's ascent.

If Number Thirty would just stay asleep. . . . Carefully he put one foot on Glocken's left shoulder and hoisted himself up until he got a foothold on the other. For a moment he teetered there, preparing to straighten himself along the wall like an inching worm, and in that moment . . .

The bellows gave a great glurp.

Scumble froze, waiting for the heavy breathing to start again. Instead, there were thumps and flounderings. Number Thirty was awake and suspicious.

There was no time to get down from the table before the door burst open and the Stickerman stood there with legs straddled, glaring at them. Under that terrible glare Scumble meekly climbed off Glocken's shoulders and lowered himself from the table. Glocken still sat cross-legged, bemused. Number Thirty gave a roar and started across the room, but Gam Lutie intervened.

"How dare you come bursting in here!" she said in her most imperious tones.

The Hulk swept her aside, and she sprawled headlong. He strode across the room, tipped the table until Glocken and the rock slab slid off to the floor, and with a mighty jerk, hauled the table right across the floor and out the door. It jammed in the doorway, and with another roar he threw it over on its side and pulled it. There was a splintering sound as the back two legs caught in the doorway. But then the table cleared with a final jerk.

The Hulk gave them one more horrible glare. "GRASSHOPPERS!" he yelled. "It's like having GRASSHOPPERS!" He slammed the door shut with such force that there was a great whoom! like an explosion.

They picked Glocken up. He seemed no more dazed than he had been ever since he had heard the Whisper. Then they all slumped down against the wall and stared at the window so far above them, with its welcoming gaping hole where the bar had come out in Scumble's hand.

On the other side of the door the hurricane of Number Thirty's breath settled down to its old familiar sound. But their chance was gone, for there was no possible way to get up to the window. Even Crustabread would not have been able to help them now. Scumble felt a pang: how would it be if they ever got back to Water Gap and there was no longer any Crustabread to live across the river?

And Wafer? What had become of Wafer? For a moment Scumble imagined that he could smell the sun-dust scent of him. But the Wafer was either dead or back with his own. He hadn't enough sense and the Diggers hadn't enough bravery to come to the rescue. So unless something fantastic happened—and it wouldn't—he and his three friends would not see the Land Between the Mountains again for a very long time, perhaps never.

Scumble blinked his eyes to get rid of the spots before them. They were bleary from staring at the gray square. Just now the remaining bars of the window had twitched and wriggled like snakes, and then they thickened. And—had he drifted into a dream?—there was a shape at the window, a round shape on top of a. . . . The blood beat so loudly in his ears that it drowned out the sound of Number Thirty's breathing.

That shape . . . and the sun-dust scent that seemed to waft into the room. . . . The shape made chittering sounds. . . .

Scumble wanted to yell, to shout, but all his poor voice could manage was a sob. Then they were all on their feet, calling in loud whispers to the figure at the window.

"Wafer! Is it you, Wafer? Come here!"

The chittering got so fast that it tripped over itself, and Wafer swung himself into the room on three legs and down the wall in a twinkling.

Silky threw her arms around him, squeezed him till he squeaked. "How did you ever get here!" she marveled.

A wild unreasoning hope seized Scumble. They had left

two of their party on the desert, never to be seen again, but one had come back. . . .

From outside the window came the soft night-call of the hooter-bird, and the Wafer sprang out of Silky's arms and flashed up the wall and out through the bars.

"Wafer, come back!' Silky wailed, but Scumble put a warning hand on her shoulder They all listened for a moment, until they were sure the bellows hadn't changed tone.

The hooter-bird called again. And Scumble strained at his voice box to echo the sound. A weak frog-croak came forth.

It was Gam Lutie who answered the call. "Crustabread," she said quietly but firmly, "if that is you out there, stop that ridiculous hooting and speak up."

And Crustabread replied, as calmly as though he had come to borrow a sprig of parsilly, "Can you get through that window?"

"We can't get up *to* it," Gam Lutie said.

"How did you find us?" called Silky.

At the sound of her voice, the Wafer suddenly appeared again at the window. He sat down on the ledge and eased his hurt leg straight out.

"Your signal," came the answer.

They looked at each other blankly. Scumble opened his mouth to explain, but his voice box wasn't working at the moment.

"The white cloak," said Crustabread impatiently. "Hanging from the window. But I wasn't sure. Are you all right?"

"Yes," Gam Lutie said. "But we must get out. Where have you been?"

"Cave. Across the dam on the mountain."

Glocken suddenly came to life. "Did you hear the Whisper?" he asked hoarsely. "Was it you making it sound?"

There was a short silence.

"Crustabread?" Glocken called anxiously. "Was it you . . . ?"

"No," said Crustabread slowly, "but there was something. . . . When I fell—"

"There's no time for nonsense talk now," said Gam Lutie with asperity. "We must make our escape before that Hulk outside the door wakes up again."

"But how?" wailed Silky. "We'll never reach the window."

"Yes we will." Gam Lutie drew herself up to her fullest. "Wafer! Take hold of the cloak tied to the bar and pull it through to this side so that it hangs down."

Scumble looked at Gam Lutie in surprised admiration. She was one to cut right through to the core of the problem.

But the Wafer looked puzzled and cocked his head from side to side. Gam Lutie repeated her instructions as though by her very willing it, she could make the Wafer do what she wanted. It was no use. The Wafer ran down the wall and back to the ledge where he perched questioningly.

Glocken took off his cloak and waved it. "Cloak," he said. "Cloak." He pointed up at the window. "Pull the cloak through the window. Look." And he held his cloak up against the wall.

With a sudden excited chitter, the Wafer vaulted down, snatched the cloak, and dragged it back up the wall.

"No no!" cried Glocken in despair.

"Wait a minute," said Silky. "Wafer, throw the cloak down to me. Throw it down. Throw down the cloak."

The Wafer looked puzzledly from the cloak in his hands to Silky's outstretched arms, finally made up his mind. He dropped the cloak.

"That's right!" Silky cried, clapping her hands softly. "That's just right. Now, Wafer, throw the other cloak down. The other cloak. Outside the window. Pull it through the bars and throw it down."

The Wafer cocked his head from one side to the other, made clicking remarks that seemed to be trying to explain that he had already thrown down all the cloaks he had handy. Then, abruptly, he disappeared through the window. Glocken groaned.

"Just wait," said Silky calmly.

A moment later a glimmer of white showed between the bars. It swelled and billowed through the opening, and those waiting below gave a whispered cheer. The Wafer shoved the rest of the cloth on its way, and the white cloak fell in folds down the wall. It came within hand's reach.

But Scumble felt a great uneasiness. The steady rhythm of Number Thirty's breathing had faltered, resumed for a breath or two, and faltered again. Now it sounded different, a waiting sort of breath, perhaps? Whatever it was, if Number Thirty opened the door now, he couldn't fail to see the white cloak hanging down the wall.

Urgently, Scumble pushed Glocken toward the cloak, gave him a boost with his cupped hands, and then grabbed hold of the swaying lifeline to hold it steady. Glocken swarmed up the cloak like a scamper, grasped the window-bars, and hauled himself onto the wide ledge.

It was impossible in the scuffle to hear what Number Thirty might be doing outside their door, but Scumble could feel his suspicion leaking through the very walls. He held his hands for Gam Lutie to step on.

She started up the lifeline, but her sword kept swinging into the wall, and she dropped back to the floor, where she wasted precious moments unbuckling the belt.

Scumble motioned Silky to go up, but she was busy at her own sword-belt. He wrung his hands and wondered if it was possible to die of fright.

At last he had Gam Lutie on her way and, dancing with impatience, held the white cloak while she deliberately, hand-over-hand, pulled herself up until Glocken could take hold of her arm and help her to the top.

Now Silky. Scumble made himself hold her foot steady while she grasped the cloak. . . .

They were going to make it, after all. His heart billowed. They were going to—

With only the faintest of creaks, the door swung open.

Scumble turned, his hand going automatically to the useless sword at his side as he saw the Stickerman filling the doorway. Number Thirty's face swelled up until he looked like one of the giant kill-fish that sometimes descended upon the hapless trout in the Watercress River and did away with them.

With a roar of rage the Hulk lunged across the room, hand outstretched to snatch down the escape-cloak with Silky clinging desperately to it.

Scumble scarcely knew what happened. The sword was suddenly in his hand, and his hand was lifting—high and higher. As it rose into the air, the blade gave forth a glimmering light that turned to a glow and then to a shimmer so that the edges of the blade could no longer be seen, but only a radiance that bathed the whole room with an unearthly light.

Blue-white sparks shot from the sword as it began to descend. Along the flaming blade appeared shimmering letters of gold, burned there by an ancient magic long lost to the world—*Bright when the cause is right*. The letters were in the ancient script, but it seemed to Scumble that they spoke themselves into his mind.

With a wild yell, the guard clutched at his slashed arms, eyes starting out of his head. With another blood-curdling cry, he turned and ran out of the door.

Scumble scarcely noticed him. The letters had already gone back inside the blade, and first the shimmer, then the glow, and at last the glimmer followed them, until once more the sword hung heavy and inert in his hand.

"Hurry!" cried Silky. She had clambered the rest of the way to the window ledge. "Hurry, Scumble. He'll be back!"

Scumble slowly sheathed the sword and began to climb. He felt—outside himself. The Scumble hauling himself hand over hand up the lifeline was not the same Scumble who had given Glocken a boost up the same ladder a few minutes ago. He was now the Scumble who had held the awesome power of the sword of the Minnipins in his hand. Somehow he knew that, though he went back to pressing fish once more in the village of Water Gap, folk would never again hold their noses when he passed to windward of them.

17

A little nose can drip as much as a big one.

—Muggles, *Further Maxims*

When Glocken, from the window ledge, saw the sword burst into flame and the ancient writing appear, it was like a ripple of bells sounding down his spine. He snatched his own sword from the sheath, but it made no response to his touch. And indeed Scumble's sword was already dimming in the darkened room, and the Hulk was fleeing.

Feeling vaguely disappointed, Glocken slung his sword back into its sheath and put out his hand to pull Silky onto the ledge. Then Scumble came up after her, and finally they were all four on the ledge, with the Wafer climbing up and down the outside wall between Crustabread and themselves.

"Be quick!" said Crustabread. "There's no time to lose."

Feverishly Glocken pulled the white cloak up and, clinging to one of the bars, stuffed it through to hang down the outside of the wall once more.

"Come down slowly," Crustabread warned them. "Don't swing out too far, or you'll have a cold bath."

Glocken poked at Scumble. "You first."

After a moment of gulping air like an astonished trout, Scumble obediently lowered himself over the edge until he could transfer his hands from the bars to the white cloak.

There was the whisper of cloth as he slid down and a thunk! as he landed.

"All right," said Crustabread. "Send the next one."

Glocken pointed at Silky. She closed her eyes a moment and then lowered herself over the side of the ledge. Glocken gripped her wrist until she found the cloak and seized it. He let go, and the darkness swallowed her.

There was a hullabaloo of shouts, thumps, running feet in the lower parts of the tower. Perhaps it would take a little time for Number Thirty to explain that someone no bigger than a Hulk child had done so much damage. And perhaps nobody would believe the part about the swords lighting up. With any luck—

When the signal came that Silky had arrived safely below, it was Gam Lutie's turn. The noise in the tower seemed closer. To be caught now, after all they had been through, was an unbearable thought.

"Hurry hurry," Glocken cried. But Gam Lutie was one you could never hurry.

With as much deliberation as it would take to pick her way across a puddly street, she proceeded from the window ledge and its bars to the white cloak and so to the wall.

Glocken was in such a scramble to get out himself that he carelessly swung way out on the cloak and, swinging back, banged into the wall of the tower. There was a tearing sound, and the cloak ripped away from the bar above him. He fell with a frightful thump. But there was no time to waste on bruises.

"This way," said Crustabread. He set off along the top of the dam to the left.

They were at a fearsome height, and the wall was no wider

than five Minnipins laid out top to toe. Glocken kept to the very center. On the right edge was a black nothingness that gurgled and slapped an unknown distance below. The left edge zoomed down to the Hulks' loading platform, made light as day by giant flares. Carts were zinging in and going off in quick succession, their wheels spinning idly in the air. Most of them carried Hulks now. Going home. What wonders might they not pass before they were put down on some faraway spot that Glocken would never see! For just an instant he felt regret for the lost adventure.

The smooth washed-limestone wall gave way to the rough, rocky terrain of the spur, and they turned away from the loading activity. Glocken glanced back at the tower and saw light suddenly stab out from the barred window. Their escape was known.

"Don't stop," said Crustabread.

Glocken, who ached from his fall, groaned and tried to make his legs move faster. It was a nightmare journey. Ankles turned and shins got barked, but they hurried onward. Glocken regretted the dinner he hadn't eaten, spices or not. They had nibbled at the coarse, tough bread on the tray while waiting for Number Thirty to go to sleep, but that was all. It was a chilling journey. There seemed to be no hope of finishing anywhere but in a cage or at the bottom of the pent-up Watercress River, and Glocken would have liked to get it over with.

But at last they reached the cave, which Crustabread had told them about in short gasps as they hurried along. At least they reached what *had* been a cave.

Crustabread, balancing on the little bit of ledge that remained, surveyed the damage caused by another fall of rock.

"We'll dig out," he said. "Digging will keep us warm and give us shelter. We might need a burrow to crawl into before the night is finished."

Tired as they were, they dug in with a will. The Wafer, seeing what was happening, stopped running about the face of the mountain on his three legs and joined them, digging more furiously than any. He threw out such a fan of dirt that the others let him work in his own corner and attacked the rubble in a different place. Within minutes their toehold on the lip of the cave had become a foothold, but there were still a good many hundredweight of rock and earth to be removed before they could all lie down to rest.

And after they had rested? It looked as though they

would have to make their way over Frostbite back to the flooded Land Between the Mountains, defeated. Worse than defeated, for now the Hulks knew of the Minnipin valley. How long before Red Carrot brought his Stickermen to look for gold or, even worse, to take the Minnipins away from their land and settle them elsewhere? Glocken dug harder and stopped thinking.

It was Scumble's hoarse croak that brought all of them back to the danger at hand. "Somebody comes!" He had unsheathed his sword and had put himself between the other Minnipins and the approaching torches. But it was evident from the way he was looking down at the sword that something was wrong.

Glocken turned and half-drew his own sword. It was cold.

"Holloa!" yelled one of the Hulks. It was the Red Carrot himself. "I want to talk with you." His voice bounced from rock to rock.

Crustabread called out, "Advance the Red Carrot. The others stay back."

The clumsy footsteps of the Red Carrot came closer. Dislodged rocks and pebbles rattled from under his feet down into the water below.

"That's far enough!" Crustabread warned.

The Red Carrot stopped. "I am sorry for the actions of my guard," he said. "He has been suitably punished, although it might be thought you had already punished him with your sword. In all fairness, he thought he was doing his duty. But I have discharged him from the service and sent him home." He paused, but as the Minnipins simply waited for him to go on, he took up the thread. . . .

"Please come down off the mountain and come back. I want to be your friend. We all want to be your friends. We could be like big brothers to you. We can make your lives easier and at the same time richer. There are wonderful things in my land, greater than anything you have seen at this poor place. But if you stay on this mountain you will perish. There is no food here and no way over the mountain. Come with us to visit our land, and we will send for the rest of your people. Come with us and be happy."

The Minnipins shuffled their feet uncertainly. The Carrot sounded very plausible. After all, if they were to perish here on the mountain, what good would they have done for the Minnipins still in the valley? But if they went to the land of the Hulks and learned from them, and if the Hulks *did* send for the rest of their folk . . .

It was Silky who spoke up. " '. . . and be happy,' you said. Do you think to make us happy by shooting your stickers at our friends the Diggers?"

There was a short silence, and when the Carrot spoke again, his voice was softer. "Yes, I see. Perhaps, then, there are things that you can teach us. For you must have many secrets. Perhaps the secret of happiness is the most important."

"And the secret of the swords?" Glocken suddenly asked. He had been straining his eyes in the half light at the dim bulk of the Carrot, and now he saw what it was that the Carrot held in his hand. It was one of the swords they had left behind on the floor of the tower room.

"Yes," said the Carrot slowly. "And the secret of the swords."

"And what if"—into Crustabread's normally soft tones crept a hard note—"what if we refuse to come down the mountain with you?"

There was a prolonged silence. "We are all going away," said the Carrot, "except for certain ones who will guard the dam against the Diggers, as you call them, and will repair it when necessary. They are . . . not gentle."

From the far corner of the cave where the Wafer was digging came a sudden ping! that raised the hair off Glocken's head. It was not the sound of rock against rock, but it passed unnoticed by the others.

Glocken took a step forward. "We will not go back with you," he declared. "We would rather die on the mountain than be caged in your land. And we will give you this warning. Leave at moonset and take everyone with you. Leave no one guarding the dam. Or better, go this minute." He glanced nervously at the Wafer's activities. There was another plink!—this one a little higher than the one before.

"I have no choice," the Carrot said sadly. "I am ordered to leave before moonset in any case. The guards will remain. And I promise you that I will see you in my land in three days. It would have been pleasanter had you come by choice." He turned and slowly made his way back to where the torches were waiting.

"Warn your guards!" Glocken yelled after him.

The Carrot turned once more, and waving the sword of the Minnipins, which looked like a knife in his hands, he called, "I'll give this back to you when you come. You'll find the other one in the tower." He strode off.

"You did exactly right," said Gam Lutie. "Glocken, I am proud of you. You sent him off with a gnat in his ear!"

"Let's dig," said Glocken. He felt as though old Thick's waterwheel were turning in his chest as he edged along the lip to the far corner, where the Wafer was sending up clouds of dust. The coming of the moon cast enough light to show him a dull gleam. He knew before he felt its shape that it was a bell.

He moved the Wafer a little way off and then—carefully . . . carefully—almost sick with suppressed excitement, he worked the dirt away from around the bell until it hung free in its dull gold frame. His fingers ached to sound it, but he wouldn't allow himself. Not until— Feverishly he set to work. Another bell was partly exposed by the Wafer's digging. It *was* a carillon, then, a small one, which meant there would be twenty-two ordinary bells, and—the Whisper?

The Wafer's dust storm kept the others well away from
the corner. Glocken had eleven bells uncovered when a sudden falling away of fine silt revealed four more bells all in a
row. In one place the framework had been bent, and two of
the bells gently pinged together. It was a wild sweet sound

that set Glocken's heart in its millrace again. He forgot hunger and thirst and tiredness and worked on without pause as the moon grew older and began to set.

Crustabread was just returning from a survey of the Hulks. "The Red Carrot told us true," he said as he stepped off the path into the now-sizable cave. "They have all departed. There seem to be only watchers who walk back and forth with torches." He stopped short. "What is that?"

They all turned to look as Glocken gently struck the first bell. It rang pure and sweet but a little dull. Dust sifted from it, and when Glocken struck it again, the pure tone echoed across the water. Drawing a breath, he went to the next bell and gave it first a pat to free it from its centuries of dust and then a full stroke. He was oblivious to the rest of the world as he played on, up and up the scale through the twenty-second bell. When at last he reached the twenty-third bell he hesitated. Then he barely touched it.

Sound whispered from the tiny golden bell, a dulcet floating breath of a chime that purled round the cave and out across the water. Its sweet enchantment lingered on the air for a dream of time, and when it was finally gone, its memory yet stayed in their ears.

They could feel the shock to the dam.

Glocken withheld his hands. There were muffled shouts, and he fancied he could hear footsteps running up and down those winding stairs. Had the Carrot delivered the warning and would the watchers flee?

Glocken suddenly felt that all was going to be well. "Tell me when they have gone off," he said calmly. Leaving the Whisper, he went back to the lowest bell and played again an ascending scale. But once more when he reached the Whisper, he barely touched it.

The very air shivered.

Three times more—fast and then slow and then fast again —he played the carillon up to the Whisper. He played until, as a background to the golden notes that poured from the bells, they heard the whine of the flying carts. There was a jangle as one cart went off. A second. A third. A fourth and a fifth. After that, the whine got farther and farther away, until they could hear it no more.

"Now," said Glocken.

And with his two hands he played the age-old tune:

> *Hear the whisper, whisper, whisper,*
> *That lost and far-off whisper,*
> *And remember, member, member,*
> *The whisper of Glocken's—*

He halted for a heart's beat, his hand poised over the last, the twenty-third bell of the carillon—the Whisper.

> *. . . And remember, member, member*
> *The whisper of Glocken's . . .*

Exultantly he struck the final note:

> *bell. . . .*

He struck it and looked across at the dam glimmering in the pre-dawn darkness.

But the dam still stood, its great bulk defying the puny efforts of the Minnipins.

Glocken could not believe his eyes. His hand went out to the Whisper, and he struck it again, this time from the other side. And then again. And again. And again. And still the dam stood.

Until suddenly—it simply disappeared.

One moment it was there defying them. And the next moment it had gone into a thousand cracks. And the earth, the stone, the washed-limestone simply went to powder and slid away. With a roar, the released river shot out from under them, roaring down the valley, roaring across the waste, roaring to freedom!

In his excitement Glocken struck the Whisper one last time. There was a sudden fearful crack! over their heads.

Then the whole mountain fell down on top of them.

18

The woodmouse queeks
And runs away,
Till her young one squeaks—
Then she turns at bay.

The tattle-birds shrill
And wheel through the sky,
But they drop for the kill
When their loved mates cry.

Remote on their Knoll,
The Old Heroes dwell;
But they snap shut the scroll
At the whisper of a bell.

—Gummy, *Scribbles*, Scroll Two
(Collected Works)

In one way or another the Whisper of Glocken was felt all up and down the valley of the Land Between the Mountains. In Watersplash, at the very head of the Watercress River, folk stirred uneasily in their beds, then sank back into sleep. Villagers in Shallows, Narrow Stream, and Stonerush woke and wondered what had wakened them. In Loudwater and Little Dripping they decided they must be dreaming. And in Fast Rapids and Great Dripping, folk were annoyed that someone should be playing bells at such an hour.

Crowded Slipper-on-the-Water always slept uneasily these days. Villagers woke and listened fearfully and then covered their heads. But in Deep-as-a-Well and Water Gap, where the fishes swam in and out of the houses and hatched their eggs amidst the floating furniture, there was nobody to hear the bells at all.

Only on the Knoll did anyone spring to life.

Ever since they had left the New Heroes at the mouth of the tunnel, the Old Heroes had not slept on both ears at once, as the saying went. And tonight Muggles hadn't slept on any ears at all. There was something in the air—a feeling —a change. . . .

So it was that she was wide awake when the bells sounded. At first she thought it was some strange trick of the wind in the trees—or a night-bird from another land that had crossed the mountains and was now carillonning in the valley—and she went out into the chill spring night to see and hear better.

The music climbed and soared, only to drop back to the beginning once more. It never seemed to reach a natural ending. Her ears straining with the effort to make something of the bells, Muggles could not bring herself to go after the others. But they appeared from their houses, one by one, questioning the sounds on the night air.

Then the music changed—changed to a tune that was hauntingly familiar. Curley Green clutched Muggles' arm.

"That's Glocken's tune! The Whisper song!"

"Ssst," said Walter the Earl.

The bells rang on to the end of the refrain, to the last haunting whisper. They were all standing there in their night-clothes looking toward Frostbite, drinking in the sound through their ears, their mouths, their very eyes. The whisper came again and again, its sibilance brushing round them, until—

Without so much as a shiver or a quake of warning, the mountain before them dissolved into nothingness.

For a long minute their minds refused to believe what their eyes had seen. Like five hooter-birds, they stood and blinked and blinked.

It was Walter the Earl who broke the spell. "It is a Fact," he said, and cleared his throat of its huskiness. "It is a Fact that Frostbite has fallen down. I don't know how or why, but it has happened."

"The Whisper did it." Curley Green's voice was itself a whisper.

"It was like . . ." Muggles said wonderingly, half to herself. "It was like hearing an echo of the long past, of a . . . a memory."

"Once upon a whisper-time," Gummy began slowly. . . .

> "Once upon a whisper-time
> A long and long ago,
> The bells were left outside to ring
> Their carillon of woe.
>
> They slept a hundred years in peace,
> And seven hundred more,
> And no one knew their secret place,
> Nor yet believed the ancient lore. . . ."

"Mmm, yes," said Mingy, and then, his voice like a whole basketful of walnut shells, "Suppose we'll have to go fetch them. The way we said. Should we try downriver?"

*

There were packs to be stuffed with provisions, herbs, all that they might need. As she stowed away each item, Muggles made a wish on her wishing-stones that the New Heroes would come walking up the Knoll safe and sound so that the Old Heroes would not have to go out to seek them. By first light the packs were bulging, and the Old Heroes ready to set off, and still there was no sign of the New Heroes. Walter the Earl had chronicled the events of the night and left the scroll where it could easily be found should they fail to come back.

Then the five walked down the Knoll to the dock. As she climbed into the boat, Muggles quietly dropped the wishing-stones into the Little Trickle. She must remember to find new ones, for these were quite obviously worn out.

As long as they sent the boat along the Little Trickle, they had no difficulty, but once they shot out into the Watercress, they were snatched up by a fast and dangerous current that threatened to turn them over one moment, and the next to smash them against a rock, a fallen tree, or the bank.

They didn't try to linger in Deep-as-a-Well. Most of the houses had dissolved into river mud or had settled into a hopeless splodge of clay straddled by a thatched roof. The sun topped the Sunrise Mountains now, its rays pointing with dreadful cheeriness at the desolation. They felt sickened and hurried their paddles to get past the bleak village.

"The flood is receding," Walter the Earl observed.

As the going got worse, they tried to leave the river bed, but the current sucked them along as though a vast mouth had opened up and was pulling everything into it. A giant uprooted tree began playing hide-and-seek with them, threatening to swamp their craft.

Wet with spray, they pulled desperately away from the tree and at last escaped its entangling branches, but another current seized them and swept them nolly-golly into the wide-spreading branches of a huge emily tree, still firmly rooted to the ground. Sheltered for the moment from the flood's fierce jaws, they leaned on their paddles and rested their arms, but suddenly another wayward current seized their boat and tugged them through the screen of branches back into the mainstream. And now Frostbite was directly before them, Frostbite and the river tunnel.

The whole top of the mountain was gone, and at the base, the flood gulped and gurgled as though bent on eating away the bottom. They must surely be hurled into that boiling mass of water that shattered against the mountain wall in its madness to get through the opening of the tunnel.

They were saved at the very last moment by another giant tree-trunk that came dashing at them from nowhere. It lurched into their boat, flinging them against the side of the mountain. They landed on a narrow ledge where they clung and watched their craft go round and round in a whirlpool until it was finally sucked under.

They were wet through, but glad to be alive enough to shiver, and the sun soon warmed them. There was drenched hard-biscuit for breakfast.

"One good thing," said Gummy, cheerfully licking his fingers, "we don't have to decide which way to go. There's only up."

Walter the Earl nodded. "Last night we thought the whole mountain fell down, but in fact there is a tidy bit left. It will be a long, weary climb to find a pass. Perhaps, actually, we had better start."

All morning they toiled, but when the sun was high and they stopped to feast on dried currants and soaked acorn cakes, they were still far from the top. Into the late afternoon they clambered up impossible crevices and slithered round incredible outcroppings. They only stopped when Gummy slipped on some loose stones and hung by his fingertips over nothing until they could haul him in to safety. They spent the night huddled on the face of the mountain with no fire because there was nothing to burn.

Starting on at daybreak, they reached the beginning of a rock-strewn pass when the sun was directly overhead. Lunch was silent.

They walked and stumbled the afternoon away, bruising their feet on the sharp stones. In the end they had to retrace each painful step, for the route they had chosen petered out on a sheer cliff.

So it was that on the third morning they started their journey across the pass all over again, this time going higher. The sun was hot, but the air was cool, and they quickly settled into the rhythm of march. It was early afternoon when Mingy, who had ranged ahead, suddenly stopped and held up his hand.

"Listen," he called. "Do you hear it?"

From somewhere it came. Far away. Muffled. Directionless.

Hear the whisper, whisper, whisper,
That lost and far-off whisper,
And remember, member, member,
The whisper of Glocken's—

and there the sound stopped. The Old Heroes stretched their ears to catch the dying tones of the carillon.

Curley Green drew in her breath. "It came from beyond there." She pointed to a fall of rock higher than the rest.

"Did not," Mingy rasped. "It's over there."

"I thought it was much closer than either of you say," Muggles put in.

And Walter the Earl was looking fixedly back over the tumbled rocks whence they had come.

> "It's north or east,
> Or west or south,"

Gummy chanted,

> "Or east by north,
> Or south by west,
> In the twitcher's hole,
> Or the wooso's nest.
>
> It's north by south,
> It's east by west,
> Straight up or down—
> What say we rest!"

"Don't be foolish," said Curley Green sharply.

"Sorry." Gummy pushed his conical hat back on his head. "I didn't think how serious—"

Walter the Earl struck his ashplant on the ground. "We spread out," he said. "Walk carefully, and if you hear the bells again, try to place the sound. Call out every few steps and listen well. Come back to this place when the sun goes down if you've found nothing. Agreed?" He didn't wait for an answer but turned and strode off, his shabby cloak flapping like wings.

They scattered out over the wide pass, scrambling over shifting stones and calling, calling the names of the lost ones.

"Sillll-ky . . . Gloc-kennnn . . . Scummm-ble . . . Gam Luuu-tie . . . Crusta-breadddd. . . ."

No answers came to the thin voices except echoes from the rocks, but still the Old Heroes stumbled and skidded over the terrain. Gradually they moved farther along the pass, until they could see the Watercress gushing out of Frostbite below them. It foamed across a great expanse of broken rock and pieces of washed-limestone. Beyond lay the lonely desert.

Curley Green's cry brought them all running to her side. She was on the slope just above the mouth of the Watercress tunnel, bending over something.

It was a little gray-brown creature, and it was scrabbling furiously at the ground, occasionally casting pleading looks at Curley Green.

"His leg is hurt!" Muggles exclaimed. "Here, little one, let me look at it."

The little thing chittered at her and dug at the rock.

"Hold him," said Muggles. She inspected the leg, made clucking sounds over it, and opened the herb-bag fastened at her belt. "There," she said, when she had bandaged the treated leg and wiped her hands on her orange sash, "that will soon be much better."

Curley Green leaned forward. "Do you know Glocken?" she asked. "Or Crustabread? Or Silky?"

At Silky's name, the little creature bounced up and down, chittering and waving his skinny arms. Then he began to dig again at the rocks.

"He does know," said Curley Green, awe in her voice. "He knows Silky's name."

The funny little head bobbed up and down like a child's toy as he repeated his digging motions.

They forgot their tiredness and threw themselves into the digging operation. But with every stone they dug out, two more rolled into its place.

"It's hopeless," said Gummy.

Walter the Earl turned to the little digging one. "Are they inside the mountain? Silky—is she inside the mountain . . . ?" His jaw dropped. "Where did he go?"

They looked all round, but the little creature had disappeared. Then Curley Green pointed. Out on the desert plain that stretched beyond the rubble was a tiny movement that blended the next moment with the sand, moved and blended once more.

"We must get him back!" cried Muggles. "He's our only link!"

They ran after him, stumbling, falling, down the steep slope. The roar of the water grew, and then they were running beside it as it came smashing and foaming out of the mountain over huge broken rocks. When they could no longer see the little creature, they gave up the chase.

"There was a great dam here," Walter the Earl said suddenly, as they picked their way across enormous chunks of washed-limestone. "That is what caused the Watercress to flood. What pulled it down I do not know for Fact. It would appear that the sound we heard two nights ago was the cause, and that sound might have been the Whisper so long lost. We noticed, when we heard the bells a while ago, that the last note was not sounded. The supposition might be . . ."

Finding Walter the Earl's manner of speech a little stiff for good listening, Muggles strayed from the others. That's how she happened to see it. It was a sword of the Minnipins, and it was caught fast between two chunks of washed-lime-stone.

Kneeling, she pushed and tugged at the rocks embracing it, and at last she held the ancient sword in her hand. How had it failed them? Almost afraid to look, she forced her eyes to examine the tumbled rock and limestone nearby. Was that a glint of something . . . ?

It was the belt and sheath of the sword. With shaking hands she dug it out from the rubble. She had her answer now, in the dangling buckles of the belt. The swords had failed the New Heroes because they had taken them off. Her eyes misted with tears.

After a while she started back to meet the others, to warn them that further search was useless. She had carefully marked the spot where she had found the sword and belt so that later they could dig for the . . . the bodies.

Heart-weary, she trudged up the slope. The sun had gone behind the mountains to the west, and dusk was already falling. They would have to spend the night in the open again. She must hasten her steps, for they must not linger in this dread place. Who knew what creatures roamed this wasteland? And what of the builders of this dam? Would they perhaps come to take their revenge for the destruction?

A stone skittered under her foot and disappeared into thin air.

Disappeared into thin air. . . . She must be light-headed. Stones didn't disappear into thin air. They rolled out of sight or fell down crevices. And that is what this one did.

Here was a crevice in the ground—lucky for her that she had seen it, or she might have cracked a shinbone.

She was just stepping carefully over the danger when, in a sudden frenzy of sound, the bells rang out of the ground at her very feet!

19

A Bell-Ringer needs must be Prompt, Tuneful, Loud enough to be Heard but Soft enough to Avoid Din, Knowing of All the Peals and Changes, and he must Never Break Off in the Playing of a Peal or Change, but Continue to the Last Note.
—Peal Book

It was getting harder to breathe in the pocket of space far inside the mountain where the five New Heroes were scrunched together, waiting for they knew not what. Rescue? It seemed an impossible hope that anybody could get to them in time. What little air reached them rapidly became fouled by their breathing. At first Gam Lutie had tried to talk to keep their spirits up, but Crustabread promptly shut her up.

"Don't use any more air than you have to," he warned. "Breathe lightly."

When Glocken played the bells to signal for help, as he did at intervals, they all clutched at their ears, for the golden tones in that narrow space were like Goldfoil's clangs on the anvil. It seemed that they might drown in music.

Glocken wondered what had happened to the Wafer. Probably what was going to happen to all of them, only the Wafer's death was quicker, if he had been buried under the mass of the mountain. Glocken thought of fish flopping about as they were brought up from the Watercress, and he thought about all the green-hoppers and the hill-workers he had bottled when he was younger and carelessly left to die in their airless prisons.

Would there be any stories told of their adventure? Would anybody ever realize that the foolish not-to-be-believed Pretends of the Whisper were true? And that the Glocken of Then had been the greatest Hero of all, for he had died outside the valley so that the rest could be safe? Would perhaps some day a young Minnipin sit in a bell tower and read the account of the Heroes who faced the desert and the Barrier and the Hulks and destroyed the mighty dam? And would he think he then knew all about heroes? Or would he see a hot, scruffy, unwashed, very much scared, not very big Minnipin like himself—a Minnipin thrust into heroism through no wish of his own. Like the true chime of the golden Whisper which cut through mountains, it came to him—the truth about heroes. You can't see a hero because heroes are born in the heart and mind. A hero stands fast when the urge is to run, and runs when he would rather take root. A hero doesn't give up, even when all is lost. A hero—

"A stone," announced Scumble in his queer croaky voice.

With a groan Glocken pushed himself upright. There had been other stones rattling down or siftings of dirt that might have signified somebody walking above their prison, and each time Glocken had played on the carillon to attract attention. It was beginning to seem hopeless. And his strength was going. Soon, even though the Army of Fifty from Slipper-on-the-Water tramped overhead, he would no longer have the strength to tap the bells. But until that moment came, he would play.

> *Hear the whisper, whisper, whisper,*
> *That lost and far-off* . . .

He heard the shout, but he didn't believe it.

> . . . *whisper,*
> *And remember, member, member* . . .

The dim light from the hole was blotted out, and a voice filtered and bounced down to them. "Glocken! Is it you?"

Glocken sagged against the wall with the relief of it. The others—but nobody else in the narrow space stirred. Dead? No, he could hear their gasping breaths.

"Glocken!"

He swam up out of the haze which had enveloped him. Hadn't he answered? Hadn't anyone? But he must! He opened his mouth to call, but the air was thick about him, and no sound came out.

"Glocken! Was that you playing the bells?"

The bells! Of course, he must play the bells. Bracing himself against the wall, he reached out with one hand and tapped the first bell. Deep and cool and lovely, it echoed up the well of their prison to the ear that waited for it above. Was it Crustabread's ear? No no, he was becoming confused. Crustabread was down here. No, it was . . . was. . . . It wasn't, but it was. . . .

"Glocken! Are all of you there?"

233

All, Glocken thought. Except the Wafer. But the voice wouldn't know about the Wafer. Not if that voice belonged to. . . . Or *did* it know about the Wafer? He couldn't remember. But he struck the second bell in reply.

"Does one tap mean yes?" asked the voice, which might be that of Muggles, but couldn't be.

Glocken forced his mind clear of the fog that kept creeping in. Did one tap of the bell mean yes? Why not? He tapped the third bell once, feeling pleased with himself. Yes, one tap meant yes.

Quite a lot of dirt sifted down the narrow shaft, and Glocken squinched his eyes shut. Was there more light coming in now? Surely there was.

"We're making the hole bigger." It was a different voice now. It tried to make him think it was Walter the Earl, but of course it couldn't be. "Then we'll send down food and water. Do you have water?"

With his tongue cleaving to the roof of his mouth, Glocken tapped two bells for no.

"Food?"

That used up two more bells.

Questions dropped down to him, and painfully Glocken pushed the answers back, sometimes one bell, sometimes two, but ever in an ascending scale. After a while the only important thing seemed to be to reach the end of the bells, to come to the final, tremulous, silvery-gold whisper of a bell, a sound felt rather than heard—the sound of sun and breeze and cloud, the sigh of reeds and the whispery push of cress peeping above the water.

"Was it a dam that flooded the valley?"

One bell.

"We found one of your swords and thought you were dead. Do you have the rest of the swords with you?"

Swords. . . . Glocken tried to think with his feather-filled head. Did they have the rest of the swords? He couldn't remember, and there were still a lot of bells to go before the end. He tapped three of them, one for yes and two for no. It seemed as good a way as any. There was something he ought to remember about the bells, but he kept drifting off to sleep. . . .

"Glocken! Glocken! Are you still all right? Answer me!"

He jerked his head up and gazed around him. It was very dark, wherever he was. He seemed to be holding on to something—a bell! Oh yes, bells. He must ring a bell to answer . . . answer. . . . It was all very mysterious, and somebody was breathing horribly loudly inside his head. . . .

"Glocken! Wake up down there! Stay awake! We're getting to you as fast as possible! Listen to me! There was a queer little creature digging around here when we came, with an injured leg."

The Wafer, Glocken thought drowsily. So the Wafer got out after all. He smiled inside. And he was trying to dig them out. . . . The Wafer, their friend.

The voice was nagging at him again. "Glocken, answer me! Was the creature friendly to you? This is important. Was he friendly?"

Was he friendly! Glocken could have laughed aloud had there been more air. He struck the remaining bell with all his might.

YES!

The mountain quivered and shook and cracked and ground its rocks together.

And then it fell down all over again.

20

It is easier to wrap up the cheese than to cage the woodmouse.

—Muggles, *Further Maxims*

Bruised and battered, Muggles lay still until she could catch her breath. Her mouth felt full of dust; indeed it *was* full of dust, and so were her nose, her ears, her eyeballs, and when she reached for the kerchief she kept in her pocket, she found dust there too, dust and three pebbles. Obviously, good-luck pebbles.

Elsewhere, scattered about, the others were picking themselves up. Around them the rocks were tumbled in careless heaps like rock candy piled on a plate. But the part where they were standing seemed only to have gently slid downhill —one would almost think that the Whisper had a special treatment for Minnipins. The Whisper— Muggles forgot her bruises. They must get Glocken and the others out of the mountain.

"Hurry!" she cried, and started to clamber back up the slope.

"No use," said Mingy. "Take too long from the top. Never reach them in time." He tugged at Muggles' cloak, brought her sliding down again.

"I am inclined to agree." Walter the Earl paused to get his

bearings, pinching his nose with thumb and forefinger as though to bottle up his brain for more concentrated reasoning. "That dusty little creature was trying to dig just about here, wasn't he."

Walter the Earl's questions were not the kind that required answers, so everybody waited for him to go on.

"We shall have to assume that he had good reason for choosing this spot. Creatures of the land are sometimes wise in the way of tunneling. In short, we'll go in from the side, just about"—and he thrust his ashplant into the steep slope —"here!"

Without question, they started to scoop at the debris.

"We need tools," Gummy said after a silence filled only with the scrape of their fingers against stone.

"They need air," said Muggles through tight lips.

They dug harder into the rocky earth, but though they bruised and bashed their fingers, they made little headway. Muggles tried not to think of the terrible truth that if they did not reach the five New Heroes within the next hour, it would be too late. It was perhaps too late even now. They dug until exhaustion took them and went on digging.

Muggles didn't know when she first began to hear the humming sound. She thought it was her ears ringing, and she shook her head to rid herself of the annoyance, but it persisted. Her vision began to play tricks on her, too. From the corners of her eyes she kept seeing movement that wasn't there. And at the same time the air was suddenly so full of dust that she could scarcely breathe. Was something going wrong with her head, like old Fin Longtooth, who had become quite simple? Fear took hold of her. *There's no use being afraid if you don't know what you're afraid of,* she told herself, and slowly straightened.

The face of the mountain was moving! It was. . . . Dizzy, she grabbed her head. A sudden scoop of dirt caught her full in the mouth. Coughing, spluttering, she got out of the way of a hurtling rock and stumbled full into Walter the Earl.

"What is it?" she gasped. "What is happening?"

Walter the Earl pointed, at the same time dodging a rock twice as big as his head. Limping toward them was the little gray-brown creature who had been digging on the mountain when they arrived. The bandage Muggles had put on his leg was tattered and dirty, and he dragged his foot. His eyes were green pools of grief. Creatures like him—tens upon tens of them—were furiously digging into the mountainside.

Muggles could feel the tears spring to her own eyes, and she let them roll unheeded down her cheeks. The humming stepped up, and the dirt flew more furiously. Occasionally some of the Diggers were inundated by the work of their companions above them; the others took precious time to dig them out. But always they went quickly back to work, until it seemed they must dig straight through the mountain. And always they hummed.

Suddenly there was a little flurry close by. No signal was given that the Minnipins could see or hear, but instantly Diggers from all other parts of the mountain came running to help. Rocks and earth went flying in every direction for a few minutes. It was impossible to get near the spot.

When at last the creatures fell back from their diggings, the Old Heroes hurried fearfully forward to see what they had found.

It was a natural chamber of solid rock on three sides, and it contained five slumped figures in dirty white garments. One of them was draped over a stand of bells as though to protect them.

Muggles had her herb bag already opened. Smelling salts . . . ointment for scratches . . . poultices. . . . They all looked so devoid of life that she scarcely knew where to begin, but for a starter she passed the smelling salts under all their noses in turn. She put the bottle down for a moment while she inspected a bump on Scumble's head. A skinny gray-brown arm promptly filched it, and the creature on the other end of the arm ran about holding the stone bottle under the noses of all his companions. It took the efforts of Walter the Earl, Gummy, Curley Green, and Mingy to get the precious bottle back.

The little injured one sat anxiously beside Silky, his greeny eyes squinched with unhappiness as he gazed into her white face. When she finally showed signs of coming round, he hugged himself violently and then ran up and down the mountainside until he fell from exhaustion and rolled in a happy ball back to Silky's side.

Little by little the New Heroes were coaxed back to life —with sips of water, with strengthening tonics. Finally all five of them, though incredibly weak, were able to wobble out of their stone prison into the open.

"I'll start a fire," said Mingy. "Make some nourishing fish stew. Soon as I catch a fish."

Catching fish was no problem. There were dozens of fresh trout flopping about in the shallow pools formed amongst the wreckage of the dam. Before darkness fell, they were all sitting round the fire and there was no sound beyond the slurruping of good trout stew. The Wafer stayed by Silky's side, but the rest of the Diggers had moved uneasily away from the fire.

As well as they were able, with frequent pauses for rest or for spooning up more stew, the New Heroes told of all that had happened. Sometimes one talked, sometimes another, but always there were interruptions and explanations tossed in, and much of the time they all talked at once. Only Glocken got everybody's attention at the end, when he asked Walter the Earl, "Do you think the Pretend-story about the Glocken of Then and the tunnel through Frostbite is true?"

"I've never cared much for Pretend-stories," said Walter the Earl, "for if they are truly Pretends, they are then without Fact; and if they are truly Fact, they have no business being Pretends. If you understand me." He looked just a trifle confused himself. "However, let us hear this Pretend-story of yours and judge."

Glocken wound his arms around his knees and leaned back against a rock slab. "Once upon a whisper-time," he began, and recited the tale just as he had heard it from his father, and his father from his father's father. . . . "Once upon a whisper-time—so it is said but who would believe it? —when the Minnipins, hotly pursued by the Mushrooms, wished to enter the Land Between the Mountains, the Glocken of Then played upon his bells and opened a passage through the mountain known as Frostbite, and through this passage traveled all the Minnipins dragging their two-wheeled carts. But the wall being thin between the Glocken tunnel and the river tunnel that was already there, it did break, and the water went gushing into the Glocken tunnel, forcing back the pursuing Mushrooms. Thinking to put matters right, the Glocken of Then played again upon his bells and caused rock to fill his tunnel so that the Watercress could come back upon its rightful course. Whereupon, the Glocken of Then sat in a place on the mountain and thought about how to get himself across Frostbite. And still thinking, he finally died. And *this* I believe, for certainly he never entered the Land Between the Mountains."

Walter the Earl mulled over the Pretend-story and a spoonful of trout stew at the same time. When he had made up his mind, he swallowed the stew and spoke. "It has the ring of Fact. I shall have to put an Afterword to my *Glorious True Facts* explaining this new evidence. To tell you true"—he rubbed his aristocratic nose vigorously—"I have always been bothered by that bit of hearsay pertaining to the dry river bed of the Watercress."

"Uh . . ." Scumble got his voice to working. "That part about the two tunnels being too close together, and the river breaking through . . ."

All eyes swung to the sluice-gate keeper, and he ducked his head diffidently. "What I mean is—the Hulks had to turn the Watercress before they could build their dam. It seems to me that they found the old Glocken tunnel and cleared it of fallen rock and used it. That's . . . well, it's just a thought."

"And a sound one," said Walter the Earl. "Ye-es." He fell to thinking.

Glocken drew a great breath. "I am going to learn all the tricks that the Glocken of Then could do with the Whisper!"

"What do you mean?" demanded Silky suspiciously.

"I'm going to learn how to make the Whisper do what I want it to! You saw how long it took to make the dam fall —that was because I hadn't struck the Whisper just right. And then when I hit it again by accident, it *was* just right— for making the mountain come down!" Excitement took hold of him, and getting himself up on his legs, he staggered back into the cave where the carillon stood.

Muggles anxiously followed, and Silky trailed along behind her, holding the Wafer's sharp little fingers in her hand. With a happy smile on his face, Glocken was blowing the sifted dirt off his bells. Then he began tapping them in turn, smiling each time the tone came true.

The sound of the bells drew the others, and soon Glocken had an admiring audience. Even the Diggers drifted back, and two or three of them pressed forward to help. In a moment they were tapping the bells and humming with delight at the sound.

"No no! DON'T!" Glocken suddenly shouted, and hit at one of the spidery arms. But he was just too late.

The hand of the digger glanced off the twenty-third bell —the Whisper—and Glocken clutched at his head in despair, prepared for another avalanche.

There was a rumble above them, but the tired mountain could disgorge only a few more boulders. They tumbled past the front of the cave and went bouncing on down the rocky slope.

Glocken took the coarse white handkerchief from his pocket and tied up the Whisper.

21

Hear the golden, golden Whisper,
That lost and age-old Whisper,
O never forget the Whisper
That sounded Glocken's knell.

—Glocken, New verse to ancient
Whisper Song, added in the year
of Gammage 885

In the Land Between the Mountains, the receding of the
flood brought its own flood of returning villagers. From the
moment that Fisher and his sons came running from the
dock in the early morning after the Whisper had sounded to
tell all Slipper-on-the-Water that the Watercress was once
more itself, the scatterlings from Water Gap and Deep-as-a-
Well started for home.

By boat, on foot, on two legs, or on one and a stick, they
went, not waiting for the mud to harden in the wake of the
flood waters. They waded through it into their houses if the
houses were still standing, or dug it out if the houses had
collapsed into a soggy heap of river clay and silt and crushed
furniture. Soddenly, they went to work to restore order to
their villages.

At first no one in Water Gap realized that five villagers
were missing. It was the silence of the bell tower, still miraculously standing, that first caught their attention. Then a

boatman from Deep-as-a-Well arrived towing a raft laden with the ancient treasures of Water Gap, and the villagers suddenly realized that Gam Lutie, too, was missing. At last, Belch the Bottle-Maker remembered hearing talk of a place called the "Mole," or was it "Hole," where he believed some of the scatterlings had been taken. That piece of news served to relieve their anxiety, and besides, about that time, a few more chunks of Frostbite broke away, and that was a new worry. As long as time, Frostbite had stood there, impregnable, a fortress against the world outside, and now the whole top of the mountain was gone, and perhaps it was no longer impregnable. The villagers tried not to think about it.

On the following day Plumb the Mayor sent Furz the Tailor to Slipper-on-the-Water to seek information about this "Mole" or "Hole." Ltd., the Mayor of Slipper-on-the-Water, recalled that the Five Heroes had indeed taken some of the flood victims to the "Knoll" in order to make more room in the village. He sent Furz the Tailor with Crambo the Basket-Maker up the Little Trickle to seek news of the missing ones.

They found the scroll left behind by Walter the Earl:

Know, one and every [for even under stress, Walter the Earl had a feeling for fitness in a document], that we the five undersigned, being of Slipper-on-the-Water, in this spring of the year of Gammage 885, have set off to find and hopefully to rescue the following: to number, Glocken the Bell-Ringer, Gam Lutie the Custodian, Scumble the Fish-Presser and Sluice-Gate Keeper, Crustabread the Lone, and Silky the Fair, all of Water Gap. Four days ago these five set out through the old gold-mine tunnels to seek a way to the mouth of the Watercress where they hoped to restore the former running of the river. This night we have seen the mountain Frostbite come down and have heard a strange, haunting sound, which we believe to be that which Glocken was seeking. The Whisper of Glocken it is called and was left outside the valley when the Minnipins first entered here. It is our belief that Glocken found his Whisper, but that he and the others are somehow in deadly peril, for it appears that the Whisper and the falling-down of Frostbite have somewhat to do with each other. This is not Fact, but Strong Supposition. We, the undersigned, feeling responsible for having sent these five New Heroes into the Unknown to save the Land Between the Mountains, now set off by boat toward fallen-down Frostbite. We hope to cross the mountain and find what has happened to the Five from Water Gap. We confidently expect to return on the third day from this, the Night of the Falling Mountain, and have taken ample supplies for this period of time.

Be aware that if the Watercress River flows once more from Snowdrift to Frostbite, it will be thanks to those New Heroes of Water Gap, and they must be honored as long as sun shines, moon glows, and rain falls.

> Signed: Walter the Earl the Writer of History
> Muggles the Candy-Maker
> Mingy the Money-Box Keeper
> Curley Green the Painter of Pictures
> Gummy the Scribbler

Three days! Furz and Crambo looked uneasily at each other and returned in silence to Slipper-on-the-Water. Three days! The Old Heroes had now been gone for six.

Furz the Tailor, with Ltd. the Mayor's permission, took the scroll downriver with him to Water Gap and presented it with fitting solemnity to Plumb the Mayor.

Plumb the Mayor read the scroll through twice and let it fall on his desk. "We shall have a Memory Service tomorrow at evenfall," he said, gazing out of the window. "Do you ask Nobber to play the Great Memory Peal."

"He plays badly," said Furz the Tailor.

Plumb the Mayor turned his gaze on Furz, but he was

looking at a faraway memory—a memory that excluded the times the bells rang late, or played the quarter-hour at the half, or played hour-long concerts until you couldn't hear yourself think. . . . "Yes," sighed Plumb the Mayor, "Nobber plays very badly indeed. But Nobber is all we have left."

And so the next day, at evenfall, the folk of Water Gap left their sweeping and their wall-mending and their washing and polishing and building and gathered soberly in the square to honor the dead Heroes.

Plumb the Mayor read Walter the Earl's scroll and then a Proclamation of his own devising, and after that, Nobber, nervously biting his lips and tensing his hands round the muffled mallets, began to play Glocken's carillon. So great was the thankfulness of the villagers to the Heroes for restoring the Watercress River and so great their grief for their loss that they accepted the wrong notes without flinching and bowed their heads in respect for the Honored Dead.

The Honored Dead, in the meantime, had been trying to start back to Water Gap ever since the Diggers had dug the New Heroes out of the mountain, but there had been delay after delay.

The New Heroes were weaker than they supposed from their three-day burial in the mountain without food or water and with little air. On the morning after their rescue they were much too feeble to move.

Gummy dispatched himself back to the valley to carry advance word of the rescue. But further falls of rock had obliterated the path they had marked out across the mountain, and he wandered for hours trying to find the way. At last he turned his ankle on a loose stone and went tumbling down a slope, nose over toes. By the time he returned to himself, his right knee was as purple as grapes and swollen big as a kickety ball. After a while, he gritted his teeth and started a slow one-legged crawl back to the camp. He composed a little song to keep time to his progress:

> "Worm squirms,
> Wild turk gobbles,
> Moley digs,
> Gummy hobbles.
>
> Crawl, sprawl,
> Sprawl, crawl."

When that got tiresome, he made up another:

> "Woodmice twitch and snakes do squirm,
> And fishes glup at the writhing worm."

Finally he just crawled. It took the rest of the day and most of the next to get back to the camp.

Meanwhile, Walter the Earl and Curley Green had gone out, trailed by the Diggers, to look for Hulk relics in the rubble. They found nothing. The loading platform for the flying carts lay under water, the Watercress having chosen that direction for one of its new channels. The whining-cords had been sheared off, and though Walter the Earl walked out past the rubble to look for the trailing ends, the hot sun defeated his search. He stood looking wistfully over the vast boneyard of the dam. There was not one tiniest souvenir of the Hulks within reach of his hands. Perhaps in some future time, when the sun and the river and the wind had worn away the obscuring limestone and rock . . .

Picking their way back to the camp, they met Mingy, who was wearing his most ferocious scowl.

"Going after some of that Mushroom salve." Mingy pulled his hand out of his cloak and displayed a deep, red scratch. "Attracts the egg-shapes, they say. Come along, then, whilst the blood is fresh."

The Diggers looked uncertainly from Curley Green, who went back to camp to help Muggles, to Walter the Earl and Mingy, striking out for the desert. They debated so long that they ended by simply taking root where they were and remained in the same spot until the egg-shape hunters came back with their arms full.

With that, the Diggers rushed out onto the desert to dig for egg-shapes, too. Soon they began bringing in the half-shells of salve and piling them in camp until there were enough for every village in the Land Between the Mountains. Only when darkness fell did they give up the new game.

All that day and night and the next day the New Heroes rested and ate and had their wounds and hurts treated with the good Mushroom salve, with steeped mullen leaf, and willow essence.

Toward the end of the second day, shortly after Gummy hobbled back into camp with his rainbow-colored knee, the Heroes had to meet a new problem. Their food gave out, and the Diggers simply and suddenly vanished.

"Just when we need them," moaned Gam Lutie. "They're nothing but a nuisance every minute until we could use them to dig some moon-melons, and then off they go."

"Not the Wafer," said Silky, holding the gray-brown creature tighter.

"Ng . . ." said Crustabread. "We might have to send him out after his folk."

"But his leg," Silky protested. "Just when it's so much better . . ."

"You could ask him," suggested Scumble.

"We need the food," said Glocken.

The Old Heroes didn't enter into the discussion, but waited patiently for something to be decided.

"All right," said Silky. "Wafer, go find your folk. We need moon-melons. Go on, Wafer."

The Wafer looked up at her with wise greeny eyes and curled himself into a snug little furry ball in her lap.

"We had better leave early in the morning," said Crustabread quietly. "If we wait, we'll only grow weaker."

They slept in a huddle for warmth that night. Gnawed by hunger, they spent the dark hours in a restless thrashing of arms and legs. With the first light, heads popped up, one after the other. In spite of the chill of the morning and their empty stomachs, they were eager to be up and started on their way home.

Curley Green suddenly gave a squeak of astonishment. "They're back!" she cried. "Look, look, they're all back!"

The others scrambled upright to see.

Sitting all round them, on rocks, between rocks, and on top of each other, were the Diggers, and if there was such a

thing as a Digger smile, they all wore one. Circling the Minnipins was the reason for the smiles. It was a continuous
mound of moon-melons!

Scumble drew his sword and began slicing. As for the
Diggers, they were so pleased with themselves that they
hummed contentedly and went on humming all that day and
into the night.

They broke camp early the following morning. Muggles
and Curley Green had made extra packs out of the coarse
white cloaks for carrying the egg-shape shells of salve and as
many of the moon-melons as could be packed in.

"Ready?" said Walter the Earl. "Let's march."

Glocken lifted one end of the carillon and Mingy the
other. Gummy, his knee bound, leaned on Walter the Earl
for support. Silky picked up the Wafer.

But before starting off, they all turned once more to look
out over the land beyond the mountains. The Watercress
River took three courses now, and already, such was its
power, a faint tinge of green began to show along each path.

"It was a mighty dam," sighed Scumble. "I should like to
build such a dam."

"Yes," said Crustabread. "It was a fine sight—to folk on
this side of the mountain!"

"They wanted to help us, though," said Gam Lutie,
gazing out over the desert through which the river cut its
three silver roads.

"In *their* way," added Silky.

"I think," said Glocken, "that it is hard to help somebody
else without doing it your own way. If we were going to
help them," and he waved a hand at the gray-brown Diggers

leaping about amongst the rocks and cement chunks, "I suppose we would make clothes for them and build houses and trim their finger points. . . ."

"When a bird adopts a ground-hen," said Muggles slowly, "he thinks she should be made to fly."

"But we could take them to Water Gap for a visit," said Silky eagerly. "Or at least the Wafer!"

But that proved impossible. When at last they left the site of the great white dam and headed over fallen-down Frostbite, the Diggers became more and more reluctant to follow. And when they finally rounded a rocky outcropping and the Minnipin valley rushed upon their eyes like a great green flood, the Diggers refused to go another step. Even the Wafer, though he made soft keening sounds, escaped from Silky's arms and retreated to his own kind.

Silky stamped her foot. "But you *must* come!"

The Leader, Master Mayor, took a step backwards, as did all of the Diggers.

"Won't we ever see you again?" Silky held out her hand to the Wafer.

He chittered and backed away.

Then Master Mayor suddenly stepped forward. All of the Diggers stepped forward—like a slow dance. He pointed to the carillon, which swung between Glocken and Mingy, then to Glocken's hand, then to the ground, then to his ear, and finally to his feet.

The ten Minnipins looked at each other in complete bafflement. Patiently Master Mayor went through the entire routine again, and his great company repeated the pantomime with him.

"I know what he is saying," said Crustabread suddenly.

"If you will come to this spot and play the bells, the Diggers will come to you." He turned to the Leader and nodded. "We will come each spring of the year," he said. "And Glocken will play the bells, and we will sit down and think of these past days."

Master Mayor nodded as though he understood and stepped back a pace, another, and another, and all his company stepped back with him, the Wafer half-a-moment late. Then, if the Minnipins hadn't known the Diggers before, they would have sworn that they simply vanished. They became a desert shimmer in the sun.

"Good-by," Silky called after them sadly. "Good-by and come back next spring!"

The way was long and the afternoon hot, and the sun was westering before they came in sight of the tip of Glocken's bell tower in Water Gap. A wave of homesickness rushed over them, and without consulting each other they hurried their steps, their tiredness forgotten.

Threading their way down the mountain to the left of the river where it entered the tunnel, they tried to make out what was happening in the village below. The square was packed with people—more people than belonged to Water Gap alone—and some of the cloaks mixed in with the usual watercress green were the reds and oranges and blues and yellows of Slipper-on-the-Water. Was it some sort of celebration? Such a gathering was unknown in the Land Between the Mountains.

They could hear the tones of Plumb the Mayor's voice, but not what he was saying. "It must be a Proclamation," Silky said, "it *sounds* like a Proclamation."

They had just reached a leveling-off place near the bot-

tom of Frostbite when they heard the first sour note of the tower carillon, followed by another and still another. Glocken flinched.

"That is the Great Memory Peal!" gasped Gam Lutie.

"But why . . . ?" Glocken clapped his hands over his ears to shut out the intolerable noise. "This surely isn't a Particular Day."

"It's for *us!*" exclaimed Silky. "I know it is! They think we're *dead!*"

They looked at each other in awe.

"It gives one an odd feeling," said Scumble. "I hope they won't be disappointed when we show up."

"Ng . . ." said Crustabread, and then was silent.

"I'll give *them* a Great Memory," Glocken growled, setting down his end of the carillon and motioning Mingy to do the same. "Now then!"

He struck the first marvelous deep note of the Great Memory Peal. It rang down the valley and ran back around the sides of Snowdrift and the Sunrise Mountains and the Sunset Mountains to Frostbite. He played the Peal through, and then he launched into the haunting

Hear the whisper, whisper, whisper . . .

and the five New Heroes looked at each other and smiled, while the five Old Heroes, watching them, smiled to see their smiles. They all turned to look back up the mountain to the top of the pass, and it seemed to them that they saw, for the tiniest moment, a shimmer of movement and then a stillness. Glocken played on.

The bells rang and chimed and pealed and sang up and

down the valley, and even the birds stopped their singing to listen. . . .

At the end came the Whisper, but now it was the merest whisper of a Whisper, for Glocken had carefully muffled the tiny golden bell before they took it from its centuries-old resting place.

And when the Whisper had sounded in the hearts of Minnipins from Snowdrift to Frostbite, as the Watercress ran, the villagers of Water Gap and their guests from upriver surged out of the square in a great warm, wonderful wave to greet the homecoming Heroes, Old and New.